BURNING ISSUES

Maggie Kelly

Published in 1995 by Onlywomen Press, Limited
Radical Feminist Lesbian Publishers
40 St. Lawrence Terrace, London W10 5ST

ISBN 0 906500 56 7

Cover design © Tyra Till
Series cover format © Tyra Till

British Library/Cataloguing-in-Publication Data. A catalogue
record for this book is available from the British Library.

Printed and bound in Great Britain by Redwood Books,
Trowbridge, Wiltshire.

For my mother

'I would burn the bloody bitches'

(The Reverend Anthony Kennedy, Anglican vicar,
    on the ordination of women priests, 1994)

Dulcie et decorum . . .

Murder was on my mind. Maybe it was Sue's snoring: you think of funny things when the person in bed with you keeps waking you up. She falls asleep very quickly, while I make nests, and lists. Lists are my way of forcing my mind into order and forcing out intrusions that bounce on and on. Tonight I'd gone from my students as a whole to students individually, those with entrenched received wisdoms and sometimes fear of concepts new and threatening. That led to Dulcie, whom I was trying to keep at bay but whose death by Brobat refused to be stashed in the back of my brain with all the other things I didn't want to think about.

I slept. Sue snored. I woke up. She stopped. Who would deliberately swallow bleach? I slept. Sue snored, as if she'd been waiting for me to drop off. I turned over carefully without sighing. The last time I sighed she jumped awake in a rage at my 'moaning' and denied snoring. In the morning she'd apologised, but it was just another nail in the coffin. Bleach would burn – oh, shit! A for Gladys Aylward, Maya Angelou . . . B for Aphra Behn and . . . Bessie Braddock . . .

Dulcie was crazy, but not that crazy. She knew all about the patriarchal power structures of psychiatry. She didn't put it quite like that – 'It's a load of bollocks,' she had once confided. 'They wanted to take my womb out – said it was upsetting my head. Well they're not having it. I said – I said to 'em – you can have my womb if I can have your balls. They took it anyway.'

She could have killed herself a lot more gently than unscrewing the idiot-proof top of a bleach bottle and gulping half the contents. How far would you get before your gullet melted? – a cupful, a pint? C for Mary Cassat, Angela Carter, D for Andrea Dworkin and . . . Dulcie.

I woke again when Sue got up at 5.30 for the early shift at the vet's. She'd spend all day with animals' innards on the outside. It made me squeamish and I'm not sure why since it wasn't much different from what I did: running creative writing workshops involves a lot of innards being exposed. People's lives can be very messy sometimes.

I smelt the drift of cigarette smoke from the bathroom and envisaged her, eyes puffed, like a baby bird's, with sleep, fag dangling from her lips. The toilet flushed, the front door latch clicked shut and the engine of her old but immaculate Beetle wheezed into life. I tried to catch the last 45 minutes of sleep owing to me but my brain was awake. Dorothea Brande (I'd forgotten her for the Bs) said back in the '30s that the writer should let the subconscious process ideas overnight, so that on waking you are primed for that day's creativity. My subconscious had been processing Dulcie because there she was, on the tip of my mind even before my eyes were open, or my bladder was awake. Bleach wouldn't get that far –

I sighed and gave up.

The dog had to be fed, Jack had to be roused for school from the coma-deep sleep only available to the adolescent, and I had a lot of homework to go through.

Daisy ate her breakfast with all the emergency of one who doesn't believe there will ever be another meal, chasing the marble-like biscuits she'd scattered over the kitchen floor in her enthusiasm. Jack, when he finally lumbered from the pit, ate his with the sullen resentment of a creature woken from hibernation. It took him an hour to consume a boiled egg, slosh water over his hair and scribble an essay on the Industrial Revolution that wouldn't have taxed a Sun reader's comprehension. And no, he didn't want me to correct his spelling, what was the point of school anyway – he hated it, they hated him, there weren't any jobs . . . He had a point.

'And anyway, all my mates work for their fathers,' he growled, stuffing homework and lunch into his backpack with a violence guaranteed to crumple pages and crush sandwiches.

Jack rarely mentioned his absent sire, but when he did I listened for the note of rebuke. 'They can't *all* work for their fathers,' I said. 'They don't *all* have fathers.'

'Yeah. Well. Where's my Coke?'

I slipped an arm round his waist and gave him a little hug. 'We're alright aren't we? It couldn't have been any other way.'

He gave me a hug back. 'Yeah. Don't go on about it. You'll make me late.'

I forebore to point out that I had been trying to get him ready for the last hour and a half. He still managed to leave the house at about the same time the registers were being called.

I opened up the homework. People's fantasies incarcerated in English social taboo; women's identities imprisoned in fictional grotesques of passivity and infantile helplessness; an irreparably soppy Cartlandese romance; and one sci-fi story that made me sick with envy.

I gave up again and took the dog for a walk.

The bird reserve serves the same purpose as the lists: in the never-the-same landscape with its paradoxically-perpetual seasons and wildlife I find avoidance. I swing up the cold binoculars, spin the focus and am out there in the horizonless bay with cormorants drying themselves vampire-like in the wind. The pipes and flutes of curlews and redshank are reassuring in their predictability, their aloneness. Even the unpredictable is comforting: a long-eared owl lifting off from the marsh, endless squadrons of herring gull flying down the river from the town dump where they've spent the day scavenging among the bin liners. All that rubbish, tons and tons of food and packaging. And plastic, like – yes, alright, like bleach bottles.

Community care

I dropped the dog off at the house and drove over to Dulcie's hotel. This was Community Careville: street upon street of run-down ugly Edwardian five-storeys, converted into hotels for the thousands of people who were homeless or who'd been turfed out of psychiatric units. Many ended up wandering the streets in the day-time because there was nothing to do, nowhere for them to go. They were seen as a 'nuisance', they got fed up and sometimes they got into trouble. They ended up in prison. Or dead.

The woman who ran Dulcie's place was okay. Dull but not dangerous. And the hotel could have been worse. The plastic was clean on the dining tables and the chairs; somebody's even tried to scrub out the cigarette burns on the formica sheet stuck to the piano top. There was a budgie in a cage, cheeping blearily at the telly. Half a dozen residents were stuck in front of a quiz show hosted by Essex man; the colour right up and his face was tomato-red. It matched his shirt collar.

'It's nice of you to bother,' said the owner. 'Didn't I speak to you on the phone – about books? Dulcie loved a good read – 'Crime and 'Punishment', that's a big one! That's the last one she bought. I don't know how she took it all, in.'

Neither did I. Wasn't convinved Dulcie did. But a big fat paperback was a nice thing to have. Reassuring, per-haps made everybody else's strange reality less incomprehensible, and anchored you to the earth when you stepped off a bus, or walked along the prom in the Sunday drizzle. Made you think you belonged.

'She had a fiance,' I suggested, stepping aside as a woman, her face bloated with tranquilisers, blundered into us.

'Excuse *me*,' said the owner, as if it was her fault. 'Well, Dulcie thought he was her fiance but, you know –' she nudged me, revoltingly conspiratorial – 'it's all in the mind, dear.'

I felt angry. 'I saw a letter from him. They seemed quite serious.'

The woman laughed. It was the laugh of years of cleaning up other people's vomit and shit, finding them dead in bed, handing over their few possessions when they'd got arrested, haggling with the DSS. She'd seen it all. I'd seen nothing. 'Oh yes, well dear, they've all got their little notions – '

I cut her short: 'Has anyone told him?'

She clapped a hard-worked hand to a powdered cheek. 'Now let me think . . . WAYNE! Did anyone tell old Princey about Dulcie?'

Wayne appeared from what I took to be the kitchen. He was wearing an apron and had pale forearms with dark hairs sprouting around blue tattoos. 'Dunno Mrs D.' He stuck his head round the door: 'Barry, did you ring the Sea Chalet about Dulcie? You know – to tell Mr. Prince about her?'

Barry apparently hadn't.

'Dulcie's having breakfast in heaven.' I turned to find a sad-faced man in his pyjamas standing at my elbow. He had a huge cyst bulging from his forehead. 'They have kippers in heaven. We're not allowed because of the bones –'

'Now, now, Arnold, the lady doesn't want to hear about that.' Mrs D. turned him round and headed him firmly into the over-heated television room. 'Did you have a special interest, dear?' she asked, without turning her head.

Yes, I did. It was partly to do with the sheaf of ball-point scribbles, the dog-eared, wrinkled, stained bits of A4, backs of envelopes, handbills and loo paper, that Dulcie had brought me each week, extolling the virtues of Sidney Prince, or Prince Sidney as she called him. They were going to buy a bungalow and grow fruit and flowers to sell at the gate. Sidney Prince held the key to her happiness, if he did but know it. And he appeared to. Only a few days before she died she had shown me his letter. It read, as far as I could make out, that he'd saved enough for them to get married. He was going to buy her a bungalow and a feather boa because she'd always wanted one and it would look nice at the registry office.

'Pope won't stop us this time,' Dulcie'd told me in her Lancashire accent. 'We're going to do it at night when nobody's looking.'

Essex man was abusing his guests and the audience roared with appreciation. Mrs D. found time, between settling Arnold into a deep armchair he'd never be able to get out of on his own and taking a burning cigarette from a catatonic's fingers, to smile fondly at the telly. 'That

Matthew – what a tease! Now dear, is there anything else I can do for you?'

She hadn't done anything yet, but I let it pass. I was irritable and uncomfortable. I wanted to get out, out of the hotel, out of the depressing streets with their hideous cladding and concrete storks in washing-bowl ponds.

'Why did she buy bleach?' I asked.

Mrs D. smiled pragmatically: 'Her bottom drawer. She bought all sorts of little bits and pieces. I gave it all to the church – tins of biscuits, tins of scouring powder, cutlery! Poor old Dulcie.'

I thanked her and went down the painted steps onto the pavement. Next door, in Sunny Vista, they had a neon sign. It said 'No Vacancies'.

Mr Prince's hotel was two blocks along, nearer the prom which topped the cliffs in concrete and dog-fouled lawns, interspersed with flowerbeds of municipally-uninspired design. He and Dulcie would have 'taken the air' together, perhaps riding the lift to the beach below in summer, and drinking tea in polystyrene cups from one of the kiosks.

A north-easterly wind crackled through the grim privet hedge fronting the 'patio' where an empty deckchair shivered pathetically. The glass front door was backed by black artificial wrought iron and a net curtain. I rang the chimes. Several times. Eventually the net twitched and I glimpsed half a face. The man who opened the door blocked my view of the hallway as if he meant to.

'Yes.'

It wasn't an invitation, more a challenge.

'Is Mr Prince here?'

He looked me up and then down. He didn't like what he saw anymore than I did. 'Who wants him?'

'I do.'

'Well he isn't in. Gone out.'

I didn't believe him, but then I was prejudiced, against his brown Rupert Bear flares and his hair: he was balding fast and had a parting halfway down the left side of his head from which he'd scraped the remaining strands across his mottled crown.

'When will he be back?'

At this point the door was pulled further open and a real smoothy interposed between laughing boy and me.

'Can I help you?'

'I've told her – '

'Yes, never mind John, I'll see to it.'

Smoothy was wearing one of those entrepreneur's suits, grey shiny stuff with narrow lapels. His shoes were the colour of old sick, all creamy and cheap-looking although they probably cost a fortune. I recognised him, despite the interval of a decade-or-so, as a once-leading light in the ruling group on the district council. I must have pasted his face onto a page at least once a month when I subbed on the local rag. He'd do anything to get his mug in the paper.

The way he'd taken over from his doorman he must own the hotel.

'Did you want something?'

'Some*one* – Mr Prince.'

'Can I ask why?'

You can, I thought, but it's none of your business. 'It's personal.'

'Are you a relative of Mr Prince?'

'Does it make a difference?'

Smoothy bristled slightly, but recovered himself. He'd had enough practice dealing with awkward questions and even more awkward people when his party went through some pretty vicious in-fighting on the council.

'Are you from the Social Services?' he asked.

'Look, I just want to see Mr Prince. I presume he has a right to visitors.' I could feel the red flag of anger being run up my face.

Smoothy took advantage of the distress signal. 'All our residents' (he emphasised the word 'residents') 'come and go more or less as they please, but we have to protect their interests. Not all callers come at convenient times, and some of them are the sort of people who might upset our more . . . vulnerable guests – not that I'm saying you would. If you could just tell me what it's about . . . '

I felt stupid, mainly because I wasn't sure I was justified in feeling aggressive about what was going on. Or even that anything was going on.

Smoothy read me well; seeing my hesitation he pressed

home the advantage: 'Is that for Mr Prince?' he said, indicating the buff envelope I was carrying.

Perversely it boosted my determination to see Sidney. In the envelope were pages and pages of illegible scrawl that I hadn't bothered to read properly. Stuff Dulcie had written outside class, when the priest or psychiatrist upset her, or Prince Sidney turned back into a frog, or the moon was full, I don't know. I hadn't wanted to know. After three weeks I'd told her she wasn't wanted – not in those words, but it amounted to the same thing. She'd disrupted the class with her rambling and some of the students didn't like it. They'd got all the marbles but not a lot of sympathy for a dotty old woman on a reduced fee admission, even if every now and then she came out with the most astute observation, betraying a once-coherent mind before something happened to shift her load.

In among the written ramblings were some poems I'd tried to help her knock into shape; they were all about Sidney who was going to take her away from all this and that. I thought he might like to have them.

I decided to co-operate.

'It's about Miss Finchley,' I said. 'I've got some of her things which Mr Prince might like to keep.'

'Dulcie? Terrible business,' said Smoothy. 'Sidney was very upset. He hasn't been himself since we told him. That's why we have to be careful, Miss –?'

'Hills.'

'Miss Hills. Not all his friends and acquaintances have quite the . . . sensitivity, shall we say, that's required at times like this. I'm sure you understand.'

He was oily, but not enough to let a word like 'loonies' slip out. Still, I had to give him that – if all they could contribute to Sidney's misery was the delusion that Dulcie was tucking into kippers while he grieved for her, I could see that he might need some protection from his friends. It didn't make me like Smoothy any better. Especially when he said 'Can I take that for you?' as if he was doing me a real favour. 'I'll see that Sidney gets it.'

Why didn't I believe him?

'No, it's alright. I'd rather give it to him myself.'

It would be my pathetic way of trying to make up for

chucking Dulcie out, of denying her access to so-called normal people and maybe a chance to get her head a bit straighter. Who was I kidding? I couldn't cope with her; didn't want to struggle with the spirals of her mind as she sought to articulate her frustration and resentment. I'd never exorcise that ghost, but maybe I could give Sidney some comfort, seeing as how she was so keen on him.

'Is it . . . intimate?' He was careful with words, Smoothy. Years of practice.

'You could say that. Yes. Very.'

He eyed the bulky envelope. 'You could seal it if you like.'

When I was about 10 I had to take a couple of puppies to the vet to be put to sleep, as they say. Our dog was always having puppies and we couldn't always find homes for them. I don't remember volunteering for the job, but I might have done to save the puppies from Grandpa, who drowned unwanted kittens in the water butt and flushed mice he'd trapped down the toilet. Anyway, I was carrying the puppies to be put down and a big, black-haired, scruffy woman with shopping bags, a pram and snotty-nosed kids stopped me and asked where I was going with the 'little luvs'. Children can be dreadful snobs: I'd looked at the dirty clothes and irritable children, at the big sweaty face of the woman as she tried to prise one of the puppies out of my arms. And I made the decision that they'd be better off dead. It seems cruel for a 10 year old, but I remember the fear I'd felt as she tried to wheedle them out of me. 'We'll give 'em a good home. It's a shame to have them gassed. My kids'd love 'em, wouldn't you ducks?'

I almost ran off, the money for the vet banging against my leg in the pocket of my dungarees. The puppies were too precious to hand over to just anyone. I felt a bit like that about the envelope. The contents were for Sidney's eyes only.

'No, it's alright,' I said again, beginning to turn down the steps. I stopped. 'I'll call again. When will he be back?'

'No telling,' said Smoothy, abruptly. 'He's been taken out for a walk. Could be any time.'

'Will you tell him I called? If he likes to ring me . . . ' I gave him the number and immediately wished I hadn't. I'd once suffered from funny phone calls and didn't give out my number to just anyone.

'Well, he's not very good with phones –'

'Perhaps you could help him. That wouldn't be too much, would it?' I turned my back on him and went down the steps.

Undercurrents

I interrupted my comments on somebody's haiku to ring Sue. She wasn't in. Sometimes she unplugged the phone after a hard day saving patients' lives. I didn't blame her, but I did resent her ability to switch off from the world whenever she felt like it. And it was happening a lot lately. Maybe she was out. Where? I wondered. And who with?

I put the phone back on the receiver and it rang before I'd got back to the haiku.

'Hello?' I never gave my number anymore.

'Miss Hills?'

'Who's that?' A male voice after nine pm still made me jittery.

'It's James Catterell. You called at my guesthouse earlier today. I've spoken to Sidney and he's pleased you took the trouble to think of him. But . . . well, let's say he's not up to seeing anyone just at the moment. If you'd like to pop those things of Dulcie's in the post he'd be most grateful.'

I didn't know what to say. It was the most rational thing to do. But I wasn't going to do it.

'Look,' I said, 'I understand how he must feel. Tell him it's just a few poems and things, nothing important, but I really would like to meet him and just . . . ' Just what? Talk to him about Dulcie?

'Poems,' said Catterell thoughtfully.

'Things she wrote about for my class – she was one of

my students for a while. Creative writing, that's all. It might mean something to him.'

'Poems? I don't want Sidney upset. Are they – what sort of poems?'

'There's all sorts. Stuff I haven't even read.'

'Ah.' Now what was there about that 'Ah'? It was a calculating sound; it said, without meaning to, that something suddenly made sense to Catterell. Tones of voice are like body language or text: there are undercurrents that subvert the outward intention.

'Yes, well, I'm sure Sidney would love to have them. Yes, bring them over, by all means. When would you like to see him?'

Things had changed. Suddenly there wasn't any problem about seeing Sidney – no problem for Catterell, anyway.

I arranged to call in after a class the following day at about 4 o'clock, and went back to the haiku. Dulcie had never managed to contain her thoughts in 17 measly syllables; her thoughts were wider-ranging, encompassing the failings of Jesus Christ, the Pope and his dealings with MI5, the sexual proclivities of policemen and psychiatrists, and the waves that radiated from the GPO, as she still called it, that could 'get up your back passage' and turn you into a zombie. That much I'd gleaned from the ink scrawls, the frantic spider trails of Biro, some as much as two inches high, others cramped into heiroglyphs and pressed so hard into the paper that in places it was in tatters. I'd panicked when trying to decipher it: madness can seem contagious, even to those who should know better.

I looked at the envelope lying on the carpet with the scattered pages of homework. Suddenly I wanted to be rid of it.

I finished giving 'constructive feedback' to my Wednesday group, decided against a last cigarette (there were nine stubs in the ashtray) and virtuously poured the last inch of Bulgarian red down the sink. While I waited for the dog to mine the backyard with what I hoped were the last of the day's offerings from her prolific bowel, I tidied away the homework and stuck Dulcie's creations on the dining table so that I'd remember to take them with me in the morning. The dog was taking longer than usual and I stepped cautiously into the gloom of the garden. She was drinking stagnant water from the bird bowl. Great.

I locked up and went to bed, leaving the house to her guardianship. She was soppy but she had a very deep bark and I took some comfort from knowing she was flopped outside the bedroom door, even if her ablutions did keep me awake.

In bed I scroggled around until the duvet was plumped around me like a womb. Dulcie'd been sterilised – bugger off Dulcie. I don't owe you anything. You were a nutty old woman – actually she wasn't old. When I saw her enrolment card I was shocked to discover that she was 47; she looked nearer 60. E for George Eliot, Elizabeth Wolstenholme Elmy ... and F for – no, not Finchley, for Anne Finch, Elizabeth Fry, Betty Freidan ...

'Sidney's not quite himself'

The university rang just before I was leaving for the 1 o'clock class. They were sorry they'd misled me, but my 20-week course would have to be reduced to 10 weeks because less than 12 students had enrolled. I didn't argue. It meant losing £32 a week, but it also meant less pressure. I'd been poor before.

Jack turned up from school. He'd lost his front door key again (his ninth so far) and had one leg through the downstairs window when I opened the door.

'Thought you were at work,' he said, pushing past me into the kitchen. 'What's for lunch?'

I looked at my watch. 'Didn't I give you sandwiches this morning?'

'I've eaten them,' he said, as if I was the biggest idiot in the world. Sometimes he talked like he hated me.

'Why are you out of school?' I asked the back of his shaven head.

12

'What d'you think?' he growled, slamming the fridge door. 'There's never anything to eat in this house.'

'True,' I said. 'There's only egg and bacon and mushrooms, pizzas, bread, cheese and fruit. What d'you expect in a deprived home?'

'I can't be bothered.' He slouched past me, pushing me a bit against the wall. I gritted my teeth. It was hormones, I told myself. Males have them too, except they're not called that. He thundered up the stairs and into the bathroom, making rave noises. The ceiling shook as he practised a few steps.

'Jack!' I screamed.

'What?' he screamed back. 'What now!'

I had 20 minutes to get to class. 'Do you want something to eat or not?'

'Nah.' He cantered down the stairs, full of smiles. 'Goodbye my lovely mum,' he shouted as if I was at the other end of the street, and smacked a wet kiss on my cheek. Hormones. One minute full of fury, the next happy as a sandboy, whatever that was.

He was halfway down the street on his mountain bike before I had shut the front door. I couldn't afford to lose £32 a week. Mountain bikes and mountains of food cost too much.

The traffic was dreadful. Why wasn't everybody at lunch instead of jamming up the main roads? I tried a short-cut around the country lanes and hit road works. As I sat there in the fumes of other cars and the blue clouds trickling up from the floor of the Ford, I tried to get my mind on the class.

I was late. The French Express tutor had got to the photocopier before me and although her class didn't start for another 20 minutes she wouldn't offer to move over. Louise Bentley was at my elbow apologising for not having done her homework again.

'It's okay,' I told her. 'So long as you don't mind.' Of course she minded. She minded having to lie to her husband about where she went on Wednesday afternoons. She minded that he wouldn't let her read books or write in the evenings – the only time she had to herself – but insisted she watch television with him. She minded having to get up at dawn before he awoke in order to scribble a short story or a poem. She minded because she was too tired. And I minded because she was psychologically crippled by years of self-denial for the benefit of her parasitical husband.

'I did manage a little poem,' she said anxiously as we headed for the classroom. 'But I'd rather you just read it.'

'That's fine,' I said. 'Well done,' as she handed me a folded sheet of notepaper as if it was State secrets.

Danny Davies was 15 minutes late. I'd managed to train most of them to slide quietly into their seats if they couldn't get there on time so that work wasn't interrupted, but Danny couldn't have made a silent entrance if he tried. He was a huge bloke who wouldn't have looked badly cast in a film about the Kray twins. I'd picked him up at the Probation office when I'd been asked to talk to 'the lads' about adult education. They'd listened politely but without any real interest – that went on the various teenage girls wandering about the place. I didn't expect any of them to sign on for floral arranging or even creative writing, but afterwards, as I had a cup of tea with one of the POs. I heard a big voice outside the office asking 'Is that little tit still here – the writing teacher?'

Danny'd been coming to my classes ever since, spilling out the story of his childhood, not grammatically maybe, but vividly. The nice middle-class people got a bit of a shock when he unflinchingly read out bits, in an almost matter-of fact-tone, about the sexual abuse and the other forms of torture his father used on him and his mother, but they rallied round surprisingly quickly, admired his energetic style, sympathised with his plight, and parented him in a way he'd never had before. I think he did them as much good, changing their view of the world, even the hang 'em and flog 'em adherents whose own sons were public school products. They had to agree that words like 'fuck' and 'cunt' were in context and, therefore, permissible, even if they didn't intend using them in their work.

The session went well, which means the students took over and I became almost superfluous except as a consultant. They were getting the idea. I beat the PPA tutor to the photocopier and ran off some pages of her notes; they were faint but as readable as they'd ever be. Just before 4 o'clock I was ringing the bell of the Sea Chalet again and wondering who gave it such an inappropriate name when Catterell himself opened the door.

'Come this way,' he said, ushering me past the ubiquitous tv lounge with its dazed residents, excessive volume and over-coloured screen. 'Sidney's not quite himself so you'll have to excuse him. He has his good days and his bad days – and this, I'm afraid, is one of them. Last night he was fine, really looking forward to seeing you. Today . . . he's in his room, resting.'

We climbed a staircase carpeted in blobs of migraine red and orange that were having a stand up fight with the tartan wallpaper, onto a landing sporting cheapjack reproductions in plastic frames of The Haywain and children with oversized tears running down their faces; even if the green-faced Trechnikov woman had been an original it would still have looked cheap and nasty. The landing smelt of boiled eggs.

'Here we are.' Catterell tapped on a bedroom door, which was opened by a white-faced young woman with a punk haircut, rinds of mascara clinging to her eyes, and an ill-fitting white nylon overall. 'Thank you Mandy. Is Sidney up and about?' Catterell didn't wait for an answer but led me into the room. It was like walking into a fish tank: green curtains pulled over the only window shed a depressing gloom in which I could make out a dressing table, a monstrous dark wardrobe, too big for the room, and a bed.

'Now then old chap, here's someone to see you,' said Catterell with forced joviality.

There was a noise from the bed, more like a choke than any acknowledgement of my presence. Catterell beckoned me closer. I leant slightly forward, resting a hand on the counterpane, which turned out to be candlewick. Surprise, surprise.

'Mr Prince?'

'Come along now, this lady has made a special trip just to see you,' Catterell patronised. There was a slight twitch in the bedding and a face detached itself from the pillow. Was this Sidney?

Eyes like rotten shallots looked vaguely in my direction. A hand crawled onto the candlewick, its skin blotched the colour of tea, and from the sagging mouth came a phlegmy purr. Then the head sank back in to the bedclothes and turned away from me.

Catterell tutted. 'I don't think you're going to see Sidney at his best, Miss Hills. Perhaps you'd like to come back when he's more himself?'

The milky smell of old flesh caught in my throat. 'No, it's alright.' I forced myself to lean a bit further forward. 'Mr Prince, I've brought some of Dulcie's poems. I thought you'd like to have them.' I put the envelope on the bedside table, standing it upright between an unlit lamp and a glass of water in which a perfect set of dentures grinned in the gloom.

'That's right,' said Catterell, 'he can read them when he's feeling better.' He drew me outside and I went like a lamb, allowing him to grip my elbow. As we descended the bilious staircase I couldn't help saying 'I didn't realise Dulcie's fiance was so old. I mean, I thought –'

'Even the elderly have their little passions, Miss Hills,' Catterell twinkled at me. It was not a pretty sight. He was a couple of steps below me, still clinging to my arm, and the effect of his neo-Heseltine hair-do was diminished by a dusting of dandruff. There was a lot that diminished him in my mind, but there was nothing wrong with his grip. I eased my elbow out of his fingers.

'If you want to visit Sidney again just give us a buzz – give us time to get him ready.'

Apart from giving Sidney a body transplant I couldn't see him ever being ready for anything, except the grave.

'How old *is* he?' I asked.

Catterell opened the front door for me. 'Actually, he's only 72, but as you can see not a well man –'

'But yesterday your doorman told me he was out.'

'Ah yes, well, he does have a little jaunt along the cliff sometimes, when the weather's good and there's a member of staff available to push his wheelchair. But yesterday, John was being a little over-zealous I'm afraid.

I'm sure you can understand why, given Sidney's condition.'

I couldn't argue with that. Didn't even want to. I doubted whether Dulcie's knight in shining armour would ever get to read her poems, but I'd made the effort. Sorry Dulcie. it was too little, too late.

Catterell stayed on the doorstep watching me into my car. I pretended not to see his wave.

The home front

I stopped in at the supermarket and bought a stack of pizzas and a bag of oven chips for Jack, and a couple of chicken thighs for me. I fancied Mexican chicken and a bottle of anything cheap but not lethal. Jack lived on junk and thought my choice of food was yuk, but I knew he ate anything if somebody else's mother cooked it. It wasn't meant to be like this, I thought.

On the way home an oncoming Capri, overtaking at about 70 in a 40 zone, smacked the side mirror on my car. Adrenalin flooded my stomach and my legs turned to wet string. I crept the rest of the way, waiting for the drumming in my throat to subside, fantasising about catching up with the Capri and doing things to the driver that were painful and permanent.

I parked halfway up the street because the yuppy couple three doors down were too lazy to leave their heap in their private carpark. Laden with homework, books and the shopping, I scowled across at their prissily-bunched nets, fumbled the front door key and let myself in. The dog had sicked last night's bedtime drink onto the mat. She was hiding on the landing, her anxious eyes peering at me round the turn of the stairs.

'Gee Daisy, thanks!' I told her. She withdrew her head.

Jack was in: the backdoor was wide open, the telly was blaring, his school blazer was screwed up on the floor, Coke was spilt on the ironing board and jammy knives and breadcrumbs littered the kitchen worktops. He was bent over his motorbike in the backyard, mending it with a hammer. I tapped on the window to let him know I was in.

'WHAT!' he screamed, his arm raised for another assault on the bike.

'Hallo dear.' The hammer banged viciously against the rear axle.

I lit the oven and while it was heating put the shopping away. In the faint hope that he'd eat something healthy I made a salad.

'Want a milk shake?' I asked him through the glass.

'Yeah.'

'Yeah please.'

He growled and gave the bike another good hiding.

For some reason I thought about the white-faced girl at the Sea Chalet. With my luck I'd end up with someone like her for a daughter-in-law. With her luck she'd end up with someone like Jack. The washing machine clicked; surprised I switched it off and opened the door (the two-minute safety lock had long since gone the way of built-in obsolescence). I take it all back Jack! I thought. He'd actually done some laundry. Bless him. I dragged the damp clothing out of the drum into the basket. The white school shirts had acquired a fetching green tinge from the jeans, and the pure wool sweater I'd treated him to last payday had shrunk to child-size. I uncorked the Cabernet and sloshed a quarter of a pint into a tumbler. Still, at least he'd made the effort. Between gulps I laid the table, made a strawberry milk shake and piled his meal onto a plate.

'Tea's ready,' I yelled through the window.

The phone rang as I carried Jack's trough to the table. I went into what I grandly call my study, but which in reality is a junk room, and lifted the receiver, noting the grimy handmarks on the wallpaper round the handset. Bless him.

'Mig? It's Gill. Did Jack give you my message?'

'No, of course not. How are you?'

'OK. Listen, we're going to Scandles on Saturday. Do you and Sue fancy going?'

I doubted it very much, but said I'd find out. Sue was

off the scene for reasons she kept to herself. I had my suspicions, but then I'm a suspicious sort. I try not to be, but I can't ignore certain signs, and there were plenty of them lately.

I agreed to see Gill over there if we felt like going.

'Everything alright?' she asked.

'Oh fine, fine.'

'Good.' She didn't sound convinced.

Jack came through the hallway with the subdued bike. I said goodbye to Gill and hung up. 'Your tea's ready.'

'Not hungry,' he said, shoving the bike through the front door and scraping the paintwork.

'But it's ready –'

'I'll eat it later. Where's my helmet?'

'Jack, I've just taken the trouble to buy it and cook it –'

'That's a funny thing to do to my helmet,' he said, patting me on the head.

'The least you can do is eat it.'

'See you later,' he snarled and slammed out of the door.

'Screw you too,' I muttered through gritted teeth.

The trail of clothing was still strewn over the living-room floor and I almost raced to the front door to yell at him to come and pick it up. Instead I got generous with the wine. While I crushed garlic and coriander for the chicken I listened to the radio. A woman had been jailed for life for killing her violent, alcoholic husband. A man had just been given a two-year suspended sentence for strangling his 'nagging' wife. I browned the chicken in some oil and chopped onions. My leaky eyes were from the onion but I dedicated them to women who can't win.

The house was perfumed with the cooking spices as I dialled Sue's number. Miraculously she answered.

'Hi,' I said brightly. 'How you?'

'What's the matter?'

'Nothing's the matter.' I sounded testy. 'Should there be?'

'Mig – what's up?' She sounded tired.

'Nothing. I just wondered whether you'd like to go to Scandles on Saturday. Gill and some of the others are going. I thought it might make a change. You know . . . '

I heard her sigh. 'I suppose so, if you want to.'

'Don't do it for me. Forget it.'

'Alright, we'll go.'

'No, forget it. I'll see you.' I put the phone down, feeling about seven years old. Before she could ring back I did the unthinkable and unplugged it. It was an act of rebellion and, in a way, of termination. In the early days I'd have hung about while she made up her mind to call back, or not. But that was five – no, six – years ago.

Whenever I'm in trouble I tame my feelings by bringing some sort of order to my mind, like I do with the lists when I can't sleep. It sidesteps the real issue, but it makes me feel better. It was 6.30, too early to to lie down and start on the Gs, too dark to walk the dog (she had to make do with a run around the field at the back of the house, on her own). I draped the phone plug over the set and gazed absently round my 'study'. Too late to start tidying this lot: dinner would be ready in 30 minutes or so. My eyes took in the scattered clumps of A4 on the desk, the sofa, the chair, the floor . . .

I carried the wastepaper basket out to the lean-to where I stored household waste for recycling, and emptied the contents into a bin-liner: two small Heineken cans that hadn't come close to their promise of refreshing my less accessible parts (which more and more of my parts were becoming lately), crisp packets that belonged to Daisy who shared the room with me, discarded duplicates of students' homework –

I stopped distributing the refuse in different sacks. I recognised that scrawl. Would I never be rid of her written ravings? Savagely I stuffed the pages into the sack, up-ended the basket and gave it a smack to loosen cigarette ends and spent matches. Back in the study I had a glorious 20 minutes culling the herd of paper I'd acquired, getting quite reckless with material that I'd clung to 'just in case' and would never need, until I threw it away. Then I refilled my glass, made a generous mound of rice on a plate and dished up the chicken. I couldn't help admiring it when I set it on the table; the browned skin was liberally sprinkled with whole cooked coriander and surrounded by cushions of soft red tomato and glazed onion. I stood the wine bottle on the table, put the replenished glass next to it, treated myself to a thick, dark green napkin (reserved for special occasions) and stuck an old candle in a stick that had seen better days but was disguised by years of carunculation.

The fire was spitting flaming splinters onto the hearthrug, but I no longer leapt up every time one hit the pile. Too late for that: it was pockmarked with little black holes. I switched off the overhead light and sat down to the meal in the glow of sidelamps and burning logs. This was very nice. I began to feel more relaxed than I had for several days and by the time I was sitting on the sofa next to the fire, glass in one hand, cigarette in the other, I was wondering why I sometimes thought life was a bastard. In fact, I felt so good I went and retrieved poor old Dulcie's thoughts from coming back as bog paper or kitchen roll. I smoothed them out with the idea of storing them with the end-of-term, anthologies I put together. I always made one just for myself and Dulcie could have a place there, something to dignify her, make up a little for the rejection.

As I tried to force the creases out of one page my hand uncovered the word HELP and then ME followed by about 50 exclamation marks. The capital letters were jagged like the scratched recordings of an encephalograph, as if the writer could barely stop her hand shaking as she gripped the pen. The exclamation marks made a sort of enclosure around the words, like a sunburst, as if she'd been unable to stop once she'd started. Above and below this the writing was cramped and mis-spelt, but years of subbing on the local rag had taught me what to look for when deciphering handwriting, and to make sense of imaginatively-spelt words, like Dulcie's 'pysisions' for physicians or 'pycheatrest' for psychiatrist. Page 33 began in mid-sentence:

> to top security Mental hospital – Ill call MI5 they can
> spy on me they cant make me show my privates. J.C.
> cant make me or Pope if thats what he wants Im not
> doing it any more – I brought CRIME AND
> PUNISHMENT today – Dovsoesky – is he still alive?
> would like to know whts going on at the Chalet –

they couldnt lock him up in a TOp Security Mental
Hospital for telling the truth the whole truth and
nothing but the truth. Dear Dovsoyeki, How are you?
Doing over there? can you send KGB man to save
me from J.C. hes making me into a film star!!!!!!!!!!!!!!!!

I searched for Page 32 but couldn't find it. My good
feeling had evaporated. On Page 34 Dulcie had gone off
on a ramble about Prince Sidney and the bungalow in the
country. I could ignore Dulcie's delusion that Jesus Christ
and the Pope were after her body – that wasn't much
more bizarre than her conviction that the entire male staff
of the Post Office was lusting after her too. But what was
going on at the Sea Chalet? I leafed through the rest of
her notes, taking more care this time, looking for key
words. In the middle of an un-numbered page was the
word 'Porngraph'. I started to read:

New Doctor today – came into my B/R with
Tranqulizs I had to take He said "THIS WILL MAKE
YOU BETTER" "I DONT HATE YOU" Why do he
inflict suffring on patients then I said. I want to go
back to Lancashire – the tranquils kill my soul so
Pope cant blame because I hav'ent got soul when
they do film me – where is the soul – pawned? NO
PORND HA HA – no wonder pychetrests have high
suicide rate – they are all sicker sicker than their
patients locked away for life – suffering – they
shouldnt take pictures for MI5 – Im not criminal
    "Dear Dovstoki
        Punish the doctors for making me sin. Sidney
knows – when you come here he'll tell you

I jumped physically as the front door thundered under
someone's fists. Jack. I realised he was nearly an hour late.
'Where've you been?'
'Out.' He headed straight for the kitchen. 'Oh yeah
mum, can you lend me thirty quid?'
'No and what for?'
'I need another motorbike.'
'Jack, you don't *need* a motorbike.'
'I do,' he said, like it was a matter of life and death.
'Oh go on mum – I'll pay you back.'

'Where's your old bike?'

'It's no good so I sold it.'

'How can you sell something unroadworthy? There must be a law against it.'

'It doesn't go on the road, does it,' said Jack as if explaining to a cretin. 'It's just for messing about on, on the beach and that.'

'How much did you get for it?'

'Thirty quid,' said Jack, burying his face in a bowl of cornflakes.

'Then you can lend me some.'

'Oh mum!' he whined. 'You don't understand –'

'No dear,' I agreed. I didn't understand anything, not why Jack had changed from a mischievous boy into an embryonic thug; not why Dulcie wanted to marry a sick old man who couldn't look after her – needed looking after himself; not why she'd walked to the supermarket, purchased a bottle of strong bleach and tipped it down her throat in the back alley; not what was going on at the Chalet, if anything was; not what Sue was up to, or who with; nor why it was beginning not to matter.

I left the dishes in the sink and went to bed. Jack was watching TV in his room and I had to ask him to turn the sound down, which he took his time doing as a revenge on me for not lending him the money.

'Switch it off at 10.30,' I told him. 'You've got school in the morning.' I kissed his forehead goodnight. He used to give me a hug . . .

Maybe it was the wine, but I didn't even get as far as H. Charlotte Perkins Gilman, Germaine Greer and Nadine Gordimer accompanied me to the edge of sleep and I stepped off gratefully.

Local gossip

I had two classes on Thursday with a two-hour break between them. After the morning session I used the office phone to call Dorothy Spicer on the paper and ask her if she could meet me for lunch. I didn't read the rag much these days since the new editor had taken over. Every week there were two or three pictures of women's bodies, some of them suspiciously young and others not so young, their thighs clamped in suspender belts, their breasts squeezed together. He seemed particularly fond of women on their knees and bold print that screamed SEX, AIDS, ORGY, CHILD ABUSE and the like.

One result was that the circulation had risen. The other was that I'd lost touch with local gossip and I wanted Dorothy to fill in one or two gaps. We hadn't maintained contact over the years, but she hadn't changed much. She'd been a journalist all her working life and I admired and respected her: she had the demeanour of a Victorian duchess and a mind like an ice pick.

We avoided the usual watering hole and met in one of the few pubs that didn't have musak or fruit machines. After catching up on old acquaintances – who was now working where, who'd retired, died or emigrated – I sounded her out on Catterell.

'Nasty bit of work,' she said, negotiating the perils of an oozing prawn sandwich with more dexterity than I'd managed. 'Don't you remember that business about the bankruptcy? All his property was in his wife's name so, of course, he didn't have on paper a bean to pay his creditors. Within a year he'd started up another company – estate agents or something. Very clever, very cunning. Nothing illegal.'

'Just unethical.'

'Right. The Tories kicked him out, although he said he'd resigned.'

'Well he would wouldn't he!'

She laughed. 'What's your interest in him – he hasn't signed up for creative writing has he?'

'God forbid. Creative accountancy'd be more in his line. No, one of my students was a resident in the sort of hotel he owns.' I told her about Dulcie, not all of it.

'I had to do the inquest,' said Dorothy. The death had been splashed all over the front page. Unwin, her editor, had wanted all the grim and gore. 'He's a nasty bit of work, too.' She shrugged. 'New breed.'

'D'you know anything about Catterell's hotel?' I asked.

'There are lots like it – there's a living to be made out of DSS clients: the rent's paid on time and people in the same situation as your student aren't in a position to complain much. What choice have they got? One place is probably pretty much the same as another and most seem ok. But I can't imagine anything Catterell's involved in would be for the benefit of anybody except himself.'

'He'd have to pass some sort of inspection, though,' I suggested.

Dorothy shrugged. 'You can fool officials and like everybody else these days they're overworked and under-staffed.'

'Is there any chance of the paper doing a story and including Catterell's place?'

'Unwin won't touch anything that would upset major advertisers – and the Chamber of Commerce and hoteliers don't like stories presenting the resort in a bad light.'

I wondered whether the nationals would be interested, but Dorothy wasn't doing linage anymore – 'Nobody is these days – too much like hard work.'

When I got back to the centre there was a note in my register from Danny's Probation Officer asking if I would drop in that afternoon. It wasn't very convenient: I wanted to get back early so that I could be there when Jack got home. These days we were like passing ships and I worried about what he got up to when I wasn't around. I thought I might tempt him to stay in for the evening if I treated him to sirloin, mushrooms and, of course, chips, and offered to watch a video with him. We used to do things like that not so long ago.

My class was scheduled to finish at 3 o'clock: if I went straight to the Probation Office and didn't stay long I could be home by 4.

The class was something of a disaster. The group hadn't bonded well and there was an air of tension. Some of them weren't confident enough to tell me if they didn't understand what I was talking about and, as a result, they'd either not done the homework or had produced something irrelevant. Two of them were persistent whisperers, another kept diving into her plastic carrier bag and rustling about in the contents, which was distracting. And I knew for a fact that one man had enrolled thinking creative writing meant calligraphy. I'd asked him if he wanted a refund or a transfer to a handwriting class, but he'd made friends with a couple of the others and used the sessions as a social get-together.

I felt drained by 3 o'clock and wanted nothing more than to go home and finish the Cabernet, what was left of it. As I was tidying away, one of the more committed students slipped back into the room. She was a god-send to any teacher – the responsive, articulate type who contributed so much.

'I just wanted to say,' she said, 'where do you get your patience? I'd have killed some of them by now.'

Without waiting for an answer she shot out the door. Suddenly life seemed brighter.

On probation

The Probation Centre was in yet another ugly, old Edwardian edifice, behind the seafront. Bill Fletcher's office looked out on rubbish bins spilling into the backyards, restaurants and gift shops; it was small, in need of decorating, and draughty.

'Mig,' he said warmly, holding out his hand, 'nice to see you again. How's our Danny getting on?'

I told him Danny was fine and doing some good work. 'Has he said anything to you about the writing?'

'I've seen some of it,' said Bill. 'Things are coming out he hasn't told me about before, things he needed to express. He's got enormous pride – it takes a lot to admit you've been treated worse than an animal.'

I hesitated before asking Bill what I wanted to because I wasn't sure whether it was ethical or not. 'Look, you obviously don't have to tell me anything, and maybe it isn't my business, but I would like to have some idea what Danny's on probation for.'

Bill rubbed his forehead and then linked his hands behind his neck. 'Sure you want to know?'

'Just give me an idea,' I said. I didn't want to learn that he was a rapist or had murdered his mother. I didn't think I could handle that.

'Well, he's done a bit of GBH, but I don't think you need to worry about him turning violent with you. Most of it's been the usual thing – drinks, punch-ups outside pubs. He hasn't turned up drunk at your class, has he? I shook my head. 'Good. He's been had for drug-dealing, but it's pretty small stuff – pot, mainly. And his last offence was burglary. This is just about his last chance, which is why we're pleased he's taken up day school. The next misdemeanour and he'll go down for a long time – the police would like him off the scene, although he's no worse, and not as bad as some. This is in confidence, of course.

'If Danny could get away from the crowd he's been hanging around with and learn some skills . . . well, you know how it is.'

I could guess. The area had the highest unemployment in the county – work was mainly seasonal – the housing waiting lists were even longer since councils had been encouraged to sell off stock – nobody was building cheap homes anymore – there wasn't much for young people to do, and the seafront with its arcades and grotty bars was always open – school-leavers couldn't collect the dole . . . and so on. Everything seemed stacked against the Dannys and the Dulcies. And the Jacks?

'I have to go,' I said. 'Sorry I can't stay longer. My son gets in at 4.'

On the way out I passed a group of punks at the bottom of the stairs. I was halfway out the door before I realised that one of them was Mandy.

I thought about that while I waited for Jack to come in. I could ask Bill if she was one of his clients; maybe he'd know if anything was going on at the Sea Chalet. I could ask Dovstoyevsky – idiot! Nothing was going on, it was just the delusion of a sick woman. Why was I spending so much energy on the dead when it was the living who needed sorting out? Because, said a voice, it's easier. Now I was starting to hear voices. I wondered if they had a spare bed at Mrs D's.

Video nasty

Jack thought the steak was a good idea, but he wanted to go out afterwards.

'Where?' I asked.

'I dunno – out.'

'That's what worries me. Come on, you can choose the video. I'll let you have a shandy as well.'

'Big deal. What about a lager?'

'No way,' I told him. 'Shandy or nothing. Take it or leave it.'

Jack could wheedle and needle for hours, and I was getting tired. I had my pride, too, and it was taking a bit of a battering lately between him and Sue.

'Okay,' he said suddenly, 'but I choose the video, right?'

'Right. You go and get it and I'll get the dinner on.' An hour and 40 minutes later he came back.

'Where the hell've you been?' I demanded. 'You were supposed to hire one, not make it!'

'I met Robert and some of the others,' said Jack, casually. 'I'm starving – when'll the steak be ready?' He removed the video from its box and knelt down to feed it into the machine.

'What is it?'

'It's great – Night Cop.'

Silently I groaned. We ate the steak – well, *I* ate it; Jack hacked it in half and tried to fit a slice the size of a shoe into his mouth. I felt a nag coming on, but stifled it with a swig of Bulgarian.

He wouldn't wait while I did the washing-up and the film had started before I sat down. It was the usual crap about invincible men whose only emotion seemed to be anger, slaughtering other men and screaming 'motherfucker' every other sentence.

'I'm not very happy about this, Jack.' It sounded prim. He was lying on the floor with the dog curled beside him and pretended not to hear.

'Jack –'

'Oh shut up, mum, you said I could choose it.'

'Don't tell me to shut up, please.'

The phone rang. 'Don't bother to pause it,' I told Jack as he reached for the remote. 'I don't think I'll be missing anything much.'

I hoped it wasn't Sue. I didn't want to talk to her, mainly because I couldn't think of anything to say that would help either of us.

It was a double-glazing firm. I gave my frank and honest opinion of salesmen who intruded on my private time, and banged the phone down. By the time I got back in the living room a young black woman was being gang-raped.

'That's it, Jack – off!'

'For Christ's sake!' he yelled.

They must have heard us halfway up the road. Jack threatened to leave home. I told him to go. He slammed every door on the way to his room and I slammed the rest on the way to the kitchen and the Cabernet. Then I rewound the tape, resisted the temptation to chuck it on the fire, and put it back in the box – 70 quid was a lot of money. I put the dog on the lead and walked to the video shop to give them a piece of my mind about letting a 15-year-old take out films labelled 18. The woman behind the counter was a mumsy-looking sort and I'd seen her taking her son to the junior school some mornings.

'Would you like your son to see these films?' I pointed generally to the rows of porn, all about the height that her son, let alone mine, could comfortably ogle at eye-level.

'Of course not!' she bristled. 'But we can't always tell the age. Anyway, it's up to parents.'

'You're a parent,' I pointed out. 'Why have these films been moved from the top shelf to here?'

'They have to be there – I can't reach higher.'

'What's wrong with a step-ladder?'

'I don't know what you're making such a fuss about – Night Cop isn't a blue film. It's an adventure.'

I laughed. 'It's an adventure alright! Did you know it's got a woman being gang-raped in it?'

That was when she called her husband from the back.

'If you don't like it you can bugger off,' he said, coming round the counter in his slippers and jogging bottoms. 'Go on – bugger off! And don't come in again, bloody crank.'

Some of the other customers were sniggering. I didn't want to give him the chance to push me, which he was obviously going to, so I left. He slammed the door behind me and stood watching from behind the glass to make sure I didn't deface his video posters or hurl a brick through the window. He'd also noticed Daisy who was barking, baring her teeth, wagging her tail and standing on her back legs, not sure whether to play or tear a lump out of someone for once in her life.

'Come on Daisy, let's go home.'

Not a bad day's work: I'd alienated my partner, been sworn at by a teenage dickhead, and been called a crank by a wanker who just happened to own the only late-night small shop for miles. For somebody who didn't like confrontations I was having a lot lately. Keep this up and you'll be a social leper in no time. Alright, I *was* feeling sorry for myself. Life seemed to be taking a different route from the one I wanted to be on, the one that meandered along quiet idyllic lanes bordered by thatched and rose-smelling fantasies. Instead, I'd taken a wrong turn onto a snarled-up roundabout with no exits . . .

Wallowing in metaphor and misery I limped home.

Tennis with Sue

Friday started better. When Jack came down for breakfast I said 'Look Jack, I'm sorry about the video – you know how I feel about that sort of film.' Before I could lecture him he said 'S'alright, mum. Forget it,' and slapped a wet kiss on my face before throwing himself on his eggs and bacon. I was so pleased I gave his bristling scalp a stroke.

'Seen it anyway,' he said through a mouthful of fried egg.

When he'd gone. I got stuck into the homework. Well, I got as far as reading Louise's poem which happened to be on top of the pile. She'd never make poet laureate, but it came from the heart –

TRAPPED

I'm only a bird in a gilded cage
But I'd like to be an eagle
Soaring on high, high, high.
I'm only a bird in a gilded cage
But my heart is a lark
Climbing the sky, sky, sky.
I'm only a bird in a gilded cage
But I'd rather be a swift
And drift, <u>drift</u>, drift.
I'm only a bird in a gilded cage
Someone's thrown away the key
Where is me, me, me?

I made some notes for her to read and sought asylum in the bird sanctuary. It was one of those soft-lit October mornings when the distance floats in low-lying mist and a pale warm sun defrosts the rouge-leaved brambles. A lyrical, self-indulging morning. I inhaled deeply and headed for the bay. The tide was out, disappeared into the smudged horizon, and the mud was massed with waders tugging up lug worm and cockles. Sue and I used to come here, before she lost interest. I focused on a group of oyster-catchers, their bills spears of startling red against the pewter-coloured mud. Among the slow, purposeful curlews were dunlin, rushing about like extras in an old silent film. I fantasised for the hundredth time about being a warden out here, spending every day with just the wildlife for company and getting paid for it, Daisy at my side ... where was Daisy? I turned in time to see her rolling on her back in the wet grass. She saw me looking and jumped up guiltily.

'What've you been doing?' As she slunk towards me the answer wafted up my nostrils. She'd sussed out some particularly malodorous fox or dog dropping and massaged it well into her coat. I made her stay down-wind of me for the rest of the walk and then drove her home with the car windows open and the blowers going full.

The post had arrived and I recognised the handwriting on one of the envelopes. Jack's sire had sent his regular quarterly contribution to our offspring's upkeep. The postmark was from somewhere in Sweden. Last time the cheque had come from Spain. There was the usual brief note on Eurocrat stationery giving me his next address in case of emergencies (ie, nothing that would involve him emotionally, but money was okay). I threw the note in the recycling sack and stuck the cheque in my bank book, wondering how we'd manage if Mark dropped dead and whether he'd made a will, and if Jack was in it: when romance goes and lust fades one is reduced to such mundane considerations.

Daisy's effluvia was permeating the whole house so I seduced her into the bathroom with the promise of sweeties and heaved her into the tub. She was sopping wet and well-lathered when the phone rang. I gave her orders to stay put on pain of death and ran down the stairs.

'Hello.' I was out of condition and out of breath.

'It's me,' said Sue, guardedly. I waited for her to say something else, but she didn't. Ball in my court.

'Oh.' Return of serve.

'Aren't you going to talk to me?' she asked, eventually.

'Well, yes, if you like.' High lob.

'I see.' Top-spin backhand. Nasty.

'So what's going on?' Forearm smash. I heard a heavy thud as Daisy jumped out of the bath onto the carpet. 'I'm in the middle of bathing the dog – *Daisy, get back in there!* I yelled.

'If you're too busy, I'll call back when you've got time.' Smash countered.

Daisy nosed the bathroom door open and flopped down the stairs, dripping water and shampoo.

'Look, Sue –' Too late. She'd gone. Game, set and match to Sue. Daisy shook herself – shit!

When you get into these games you have to really want to resolve things in order to stop arsing around. What I wanted at that moment was to get Daisy back into the bath. I dragged her up the stairs and finished the job, and thought how it was too early to finish the Bulgarian and too late to do anything about Sue and me.

Scandles

Scandles [sic joke] was yet another converted Edwardian professional man's castle, and he'd be spinning in his grave if he could see it now. The basement had been knocked through and turned into a disco. When you couldn't take the noise any more you retreated to the ground-floor where there was a bar and lounge. Above that the house was private, forbidden territory to all but the few honoured by Beeb and Ivor, who owned the place. Beeb was a tall, skinny, comfortable-looking man who always wore baggy brown corduroys and hound-stooth shirts. He had a faintly absent-minded air as if he was thinking of something else, but he was warmly indulgent of his customers, patting their hands gently and nodding a lot while they told him the latest joke he'd heard a hundred times before, or sobbed into their beer. He was never offended – probably because he never listened to what anyone said. If there was a drama in the loo, Beeb would lollop in on his giraffe legs and persuade heart-broken lovers not to drown themselves in the basin, or re-arrange the dental work of a rival.

Ivor liked chains and leather, wore a privet-sized moustache and used depilatories on his scalp. If Beeb failed to restore order to the premises, Ivor was an expert pacifier with the arm-lock. They didn't get much trouble – less than the straight bars on the seafront, that's for sure.

The place was packed. Like all the night clubs I've ever been to, gay or gutty, it had that air of almost desperate hedonism, that tomorrow-we-may-be-dead determination that characterises Saturday nights on the town. Ellie was bopping away on the dancefloor when I descended with my drink. Strobes flickered on the dancers making them look more frenetic than the crowded floor allowed. I joined Gill at a table.

'No Sue?' she shouted.

I stuck my mouth close to her ear: 'We're not talking.'

'Again!'

I shrugged and held out my hands, palms upwards.

We sat under the blanket of sound, watching the

struggle for self-expression on the dancefloor. For maybe 20 minutes there wasn't break in the din and I declined to dance, content to watch my friends do their thing. Content wasn't quite the right word: it took half a bottle of plonk and, ideally, a joint to get me uninhibited enough to lose myself in the dance, which was why I usually got stoned and what annoyed Sue, who wasn't self-conscious and was deeply hostile to mind-control drugs. It was this self-assurance that had appealed to me – clarity of purpose is a magnet to ditherers, and Sue's nerveless enthusiasm was dangerous and attractive. It hadn't surprised me that she'd been a member of the Communist Party or that she'd been arrested on a CND march in the 60s. It did surprise me when I found it so seductive after years of carefully-nurtured fence-sitting. I used to watch her from my usual sideline with a mixture of suspicion and admiration: she was either mad or one of the sanest people I'd met. It eventually dawned on me with the subtlety of a pickaxe hitting a powerline that I not only admired her but had fallen in love. My response had been typical: instead of enjoying the sensation I'd felt angry at letting myself get hooked. Love was a mug's game that, after Mark, I'd promised myself I wouldn't play again. I didn't need anybody and I wasn't good at it anyway.

I went upstairs for another drink. Damn her! Tonight was my night. Jack was sleeping at a friend's, I'd had a shitty week, and I wanted to blot out dreariness, dickheads, Dulcie and – me. I ordered two glasses of medium dry white, downed one at the bar, and took the other back to the dance.

Ellie flung her arms around me in a sisterly hug and grinned her huge grin, showing her teeth and gums and not giving a damn.

'How y'doing, Mig?'

'Okay,' I screeched, hugging her. Ellie's a one-off: big, generous, funny. Good photographer, too.

'Where's Sue?' When I shook my head she said 'Aah' and gave me another squeeze.

Half a bottle of plonk later I was on the floor and swinging away with the rest of them, happy to be with women I cared for, women I'd shared a lot with, women.

I was, shall we say, mellow . . .

In the loo, a familiar face appeared over my shoulder, reflected in the wash-basin mirror. It was Reva; red-haired, green-eyed Reva, whose mother was an Egyptian. 'Hi,' she said.

We danced. So what! Alright, it was a slow number; and, alright, Gill caught my eye meaningfully. I didn't have to justify myself. For all I knew, Sue was in bed right at this very moment – this moment with Reva pressed into me like goldleaf on a book cover – this very moment, with that good-looking policewoman, her with the bleach-blonde hair. Bleach. There was that word again. Reva's hand slid up my back, under my hair.

'Can I cut in?'

Gill's face swam into view over Reva's shoulder. And behind her, further back, another face, just glimpsed as the music stopped. I was still looking for it as Reva stepped aside and Gill propelled me upstairs. She left me in a swirl of conversation and shouldered her way to the bar. I was watching the crowd coming up the stairs and out the front door or cramming into the lounge.

'Quick – get a table – there's one over there.' Balancing two glasses in one hand and cupping my elbow with the other – who else had done that recently? – Gill ferried me to a chair. 'Looking for someone?' she asked, pointedly. She probably thought the someone was Reva. But she was wrong. I lifted the glass, more in a salute to my brief encounter with self-forgetfulness than with the intention of re-establishing it. Mandy's deadly white face had put paid to that.

Beeb was emptying ashtrays and I tugged at his sleeve as he passed our table. He and Ivor had a policy of never passing on information about club members; you never knew who might be asking. Tonight was no different. No, he didn't know anything about a white-faced punk called Mandy. So long as she signed in, paid her entrance fee, didn't deal on the premises or cause annoyance to the customers, she had a right to her privacy.

Gill, who used Scandles more frequently than I did, had seen her several times, always in the company of men, but she didn't know anything about her. She wanted to know why I was so interested, and I made some lame excuse about the rarity of finding a punk in a place like Scandles.

Reva was leaving with someone else. She didn't look my way – she'd probably forgotten me already and that suited me fine. I'd have hated myself in the morning. I think. As it was, I felt quite virtuous the next day. Whatever Sue'd been up to, I hadn't, even if it had taken a little help from my friends to keep me on the not-exactly-straight but certainly the narrow. I cleared the backlog of homework, did the housework, walked Daisy, and read the Observer while dinner cooked. Jack actually ate most of the meal, except the sprouts which, as he so delicately put it, made him 'throw up'. He went to bed before 10.30 and I sat by the fire for another half-hour feeling I belonged to the nice middle-class life of happy families to which we are encouraged to aspire. Even if it is a myth.

Saint Catterell

After my class on Monday I phoned Bill Fletcher and asked him about Mandy on the pretext that I had a couple of vacancies in my women-only writing workshop and was scouting around for unwaged women who might like a free enrolment. Mandy wasn't his client, but he put me through to her PO. She sounded doubtful.

'I'll ask Mandy when I see her tomorrow if you like, but you ought to know she's dyslexic and she doesn't communicate well in groups. Did Bill tell you she's a registered addict? More often than not she's off the planet. I probably shouldn't tell you that, but if she joins your class you'll need to know. She can be almost impossible to get through to sometimes. And she's not actually unwaged – she has a job.'

I said I knew, having seen her at the Sea Chalet: 'Do many of your clients work in those hotels?'

'Hostels,' she corrected. 'Unfortunately, no – the chap

who runs it is one of the few prepared to take on kids like Mandy. He doesn't pay much but at least he gives them a regular income and a bit of self-respect.' One up to Catterell, I thought. 'A lot of the hoteliers around here complain about teenagers, but they don't want to do anything about it. They just want them out of sight so the summer visitors aren't offended or inconvenienced. I wish there were more employers like Mr Catterell.'

It was me who was the creep, not Catterell: I didn't want Mandy in my class, any more than I'd wanted Dulcie. I might criticise the hoteliers, but I wasn't any better. I made up some tatty excuse about an income limit that would exclude her from eligibility for a place. The PO asked how much it would cost and I told her £52.

'She wouldn't get much more than that a week, what with the free meals – anyway she doesn't always turn up for work. I'm surprised she hasn't been sacked.'

Saint Catterell's halo grew bigger.

'Perhaps it wouldn't work,' I said. 'It was just an idea.'

'Good of you to bother,' said the PO. 'Most people don't want to know.'

I drove, telling myself I couldn't cope – and had a right not to – *and* Mandy wouldn't want to enrol anyway et cetera. On the way I parked in town and went to the Post Office to collect my one-parent child benefit, joining the queue of women clutching their yellow books with which they were either zapping fractious children or fanning away the stench from a bag-lady whose feet were wrapped in bin-liners held on with rubber bands. There was an obvious gap between her and the queuers either side which she constantly shuffled to fill only to have the gap increase as soon as she got close.

Outside it was raining. I went over to the bank and paid in Mark's cheque. I did think of asking for a balance, but chickened out: what I didn't know couldn't hurt me.

And with that comforting homily in mind I put behind me the Sea Chalet and all its incumbents, dead or alive.

Party time

Dulcie stopped haunting me, Jack was almost humane, the bank manager invited me to increase my Credit Zone, and Sue and I were talking. Nothing else, but you can't have everything. I came clean to going to Scandles without her – she'd find out anyway – and told her it hadn't been much fun without her, which it wasn't. I didn't ask her any questions because I didn't want to be told any lies, and we were both very philosophical about the relationship. Maybe because it didn't matter as much as it used to, but what did we expect after six years? We saw ourselves slipping gracefully into late middle-age, free of all the grand passions that became nothing more than a pain in the neck; two adults in a comfortable, undemanding relationship. Jack would be up and away soon and we would think about sharing the housework and expenses and the evenings by the fireside.

Bandaged in euphoria I snuggled into my rut. The list of heroines hadn't developed past G, my classes were proceeding at a respectable pace with minimal fall-off, and I wasn't even allowing the advent of Christmas a toe-hold in my consciousness or my bank balance. The Wednesday group, angry with the university's threat to close their class, decided to form their own writing circle and meet in each other's homes once a week in the New Year. I agreed to join them every now and then to have a look at their work. So that was alright. Further afield the world was disembowelling itself: Eastern Europeans were killing one another, the Middle East was messier than ever, babies were starving to death in the forgotten famine zones, and unemployment in Britain was over the three million mark. But if you didn't read the papers, or switch on the television news, or talk to anybody who was both intelligent and angry, you could keep it at bay. For a bit.

Towards the end of November we were invited to a party. Sue was in her sociable mode so we went. The hostess was a glib, complacent woman who was neither intelligent nor angry about the state of the world but who threw interesting parties because she knew everybody and they knew her. And if she did have a scented candle-lit shrine to Margaret Thatcher in her bedroom, I didn't have to pay homage to it because I hadn't been in it and hadn't any intentions of doing so. Mira's bookshelves were lined with expensive hardbacks extolling the virtues of sado-masochism and you could usually find a knot of partygoers huddled over the coffee table muttering 'Bloody hell!' and 'That's not possible!' while thumbing the glossy pages. Mira was nothing but a dirty old woman with values that a beer-bellied Rambo addict would have understood, but I was still in my judge-them-not phase and Sue and I were celebrating a return to equanimity, so we both shut our eyes and minds to Mira's proclivities and joined the dance. We stayed out of the porn corner, out of the kitchen where some diesels were posing as good ol' gals, and out of trouble.

I don't know at what point I noticed Mandy. The door to the stairs had been opening and shutting all night for newcomers, so she could have arrived at any time. Towards midnight there must have been close on 80 people in Mira's rambling apartment, and the air was thick with the smoke of spliffs and legals. The white face swam into view and then out.

'Who's that?' Sue asked, following my look.

I told as much as I was prepared to, which wasn't much. She seemed satisfied and got up to dance with Ellie and Maureen. Mandy seemed to be on her own and was obviously stoned, a lonely figure, wafting between the drinks table and the dance area where her skinny legs in their black tights worked her Doc Martens to a differ-ent rhythm than the one coming out of the tape deck. One of the younger men who was a good dancer started to move with her, but she didn't even notice. Sue dragged me into the dance and I lost sight of Mandy, until much later when I paid a visit to the lavatory. It was crowded but I happened to know that Mira's flat included a second loo, so I worked my way through the throng to the other side of the apartment, into a hallway that had been converted into a bathroom. It was carpeted in deep rose pink with a round sunken bath more or less in the middle. And it was already occupied. Slumped beside the expensive flowered toilet bowl, one leg draped across a massive wickerwork panier in which Mira had artfully arranged multi-coloured toilet rolls, was Mandy, her white face staring out of the acres of Axeminster. Her other leg was exposed to halfway up the thigh around which a length of rubber tubing was tightly tied. I knelt down beside her and released the tubing, wondering what to do about the hypodermic sticking out of a hole in her leg. I searched the hypochondriac-size medicine cabinet above the toilet bowl and then spotted a pair of Marigolds behind the cystern. I put them on before removing the syringe and dabbing off a bead of blood with Mira's cotton wool balls.

'Mandy, are you alright?'

She murmured something unintelligible.

I pulled her up and propped her against the toilet. Her head lolled back and her eyeballs slid up until only the lower half of her pupils was showing. I pushed back one of the sleeves on her bomber jacket and tried to find a pulse, but there was a lot of scar tissue on both wrists and I wasn't sure whether it was my pulse I was feeling or hers. I left her propped up like a Guy Fawkes dummy and went to get Mira, who was less than thrilled to find a junkie crashed out in her private bathroom.

'It's what comes of letting in people like that' (she said 'people' like she meant 'vermin'). 'You'll have to get her out – I can't have the police being called.' No, that wouldn't go down too well with the law firm she worked for.

'You can't just chuck her out onto the street – what if she's OD'd? She could die.'

Mira wasn't too bothered about the demise of a dope-head, but she could see that the repurcussions would be worse if a death was traced back to her premises.

'Alright, you stay with her,' she ordered, looking with distaste at me and Mandy. 'Bob Brenchley's a doctor – he'll know if she's alright or not. And don't let anybody in.'

It seemed like half an hour but could only have been minutes before Mira returned with one of her guests, carefully locking the bathroom door behind her. While he checked Mandy over, Mira wrung her hands and whinged about people taking liberties with her generosity. She wasn't going to give parties if people made this sort of trouble. After all, nobody minded a joint or two, but mainlining was something else, and what about the carpet? – and couldn't Bob get a hurry-on? Brenchley didn't seem to be in a hurry to put Mira out of her misery. He sent her out to get his bag from his car boot.

'Is she going to be alright?' I asked him.

'Oh, I think so. It's a combination of the booze and this.' He indicated the syringe which I'd put on the side of the bath. 'Do you know how much she injected?' I shook my head. 'I wonder where she prepared it – there doesn't seem to be any gear about,' Brenchley mused. He put his hands under Mandy's armpits in order to pull her forward so he could look behind the toilet. 'Nope. Must have been one she prepared earlier.'

Mira returned with the bag, squeezing round the bathroom door so that none of the guests could see in. She was out of breath and flustered. 'Can she go now – can you get her up?'

Brenchley ignored her and pulled a stethoscope from his bag.

'She can't stay here,' Mira persisted. 'Can't you take her in your car?'

'Mira, love,' said Brenchley without looking at her, 'be a good girl and go and make some coffee.'

I didn't mind Mira being patronised by a man. She was probably used to it anyway, if not in such a dismissive way.

I stayed with Brenchley while he listened to and touched Mandy's body. He slapped her lightly a couple of times round the face, talked to her and tried to get her to respond. After an age she managed a grunt and then a 'Yes' when he asked her if she could hear him. Then he dabbled in his case and came out with a hypodermic and a small bottle from which he filled the needle.

'Now,' he muttered, more to himself than me, 'let's see if we find a vein that we can get into.' It wasn't easy: Mandy's arms were a warzone of scabs and scars. I looked away as he pierced the ruined skin. 'Okay, let's

41

see what that does,' he said, sitting back on the carpet.

We watched Mandy as she slowly twitched and coughed back to what we choose to call life. It didn't seem a hell of an improvement on where she was ten minutes ago, but Brenchley appeared to be satisfied.

'Is she with you?' he asked, looking at me for the first time.

'I think she came on her own.'

'Well, she'll need someone to stay with her for a bit, in case she vomits and chokes on it. Then she ought to be taken home.'

'She hasn't taken an overdose then? Is she going to be alright?'

Brenchley shrugged. 'Look at her – it's only a question of time. How old d'you think she is?'

'Eighteen, nineteen?'

'She won't make 20 at this rate,' he said.

We contemplated Mandy while she struggled back to consciousness – or struggled against it. Mira returned with two mugs of coffee. 'Who's it for?' she asked irritably. Brenchley took both mugs from her, handed one to me, drank from the other and pulled a face. He held the mug in front of Mandy's glazed eyes: 'Come on, have a sip,' he said, clamping both her hands round the mug and helping it to her mouth. The liquid ran down her fingers and onto the carpet. Before Mira could dive in with the nearest bath sponge, Brenchley pointed to the syringe on the edge of the bath. 'Get rid of that – and be careful. One prick, Mira, and you could catch God knows what.' He grinned at me as he rose to his feet: 'Couldn't have Mira getting a prick, could we. I'll be outside for . . . another 20 minutes or so. If you want me come and get me.'

'But what about her?' Mira whined.

Brenchley flung an arm round her shoulders and headed her towards the door. 'Don't worry Mira – you won't have a corpse on your hands. Just leave her for a bit – and *then* you can kick her out.'

Our hostess shot me a baleful glance. 'I want her out of here as soon as she can walk. And don't bring that sort of . . . ' she was lost for words.

'Person?' I suggested.

'Rubbish,' she spat, 'that sort of rubbish. I wouldn't have let you through the door if I'd known. I don't know you anyway – who are you? – never mind, don't bother – I don't want to know.'

There wasn't much point protesting. I didn't care if I never got invited to another party in my life, certainly not by Mira.

'Would you tell Sue where I am?' I asked 'She'll be wondering.'

'Who's Sue?' Mira snarled, slamming the door behind her.

I leaned back against the wall and shut my eyes against the insistent pink. The music from the lounge was reduced to a distant thudding that kept time with the pain just above my left eye.

'Wannago.'

I opened my eyes to see Mandy lurching to her feet, the mug tumbling down her body onto the pastel toilet rolls.

'Okay, just go easy. We'll get you home.' I slipped an arm under her shoulders and we stumbled back to the party. I dumped Mandy on a chair – 'Don't move, I'll be back. I just have to find someone.'

'Where the hell have you been?' said Sue.

'Hell's close. There's a poor girl who needs taking home.'

Sue's eyes glittered as only Sue's eyes could. 'So why do *you* have to take her?'

I wasn't in the mood for a fight. 'Are you going to help me or not?'

Between us we got Mandy down the unending stairs and into Sue's car which was parked a thousand miles away. It was raining heavily and a really shitty wind was blowing off the seafront. I prayed that Mandy didn't throw up in the Beetle.

'Where to?' Sue's voice had taken on that iron-hard edge that I knew from experience wouldn't soften until it had either dented my armour or been worn down by a couple of days of non-communication.

I asked Mandy where she wanted to go, my voice sounding embarrassingly brittle in the tense atmosphere. Mandy responded by trying to get out of the car and I had to drag her back. Sue's eyes struck sparks off the driving mirror. I made 'it'll be alright' noises, feeling a complete nerd, and wedged Mandy firmly between me and the seat, endeavouring to lash her in with the safety belt. I'll laugh about this one day, I thought. Sue won't, but I might.

We ended up on one of the vast estates that littered the perimeter of town. Orange street lamps bled their sickly glow over ramshackle fences and neglected gardens. Endless identical houses stretched on and on down potholed roads lined with Cortinas and rusting Jaguars. There was an indifferent air about the estate, as if it shut out the likes of me and shut in the likes of them.

'So where is it?' Sue demanded, of me, not Mandy.

'Do here,' our passenger mumbled. I looked out of the window. We were outside a row of shops: a kebab take-away was still open at – I leant forward to see the dashboard clock and heard Sue give a deep and menacing sigh – at 1.35. Next to it was a bookies, a newsagents and an off-licence that sold videos.

'You sure? Here?'

'Yeah. Thanks.' I started to ask her if she wanted me to go with her, but she was out of the car and onto the pavement. A taxi driver got out of his cab, said something to her, then took her by the arm into the kebab house. She wasn't completely steady on her feet, but she'd made a quicker recovery than I'd thought possible.

I got out of the back and into the front passenger seat. Sue maintained an ominous silence all the way home.

'Coming in?' I asked.

'If you want.'

It was too late to make amends, and I wasn't even sure what for. 'Up to you,' I said, opening the door.

'Don't bother,' said Sue, and drove off.

As soon as I lay down in bed my brain decided to engage itself. I turned onto my stomach and pushed my pillow away. H for Hite, Octavia Hill, Winifred Holtby, Hecuba, Hecate, Harriet Harman, Caroline Herschel . . . I for Celia Imrie . . . and – J for Jezebel, Sophia Jex-Blake, June Jordan, Katy Jurado and somebody Jackson. Who was she? She was a policewoman.

Revelations

Term ended with the usual Christmas stories, candle-light and crisps. I spent a week preparing anthologies of students' work on the photocopier and trying not to think about the expense of the forthcoming orgy. Jack would want money – he'd finally outgrown the pillowcase under the tree. It was sad in a way, and I was glad in a way: searching for gifts on a limited income wasn't my idea of fun. About this time of the year I started to have night-mares about it being five minutes before closing on Christmas Eve and I'd forgotten to buy anything. In one sweat-making dream I ended up in the Co-op with shelves empty of everything except teddy bears.

I was maintaining a posture of brittle humour as a means of handling Sue's absence from my life. I'd had reports of her being seen around with the younger and unmentionable – well, her anyway, but I couldn't work up the energy to get angry about it. Maybe it was just well. Our women friends were hurt, as if she'd betrayed them instead of me, and I was secretly enjoying the mar-tyrdom, stoically brushing aside their commiserations. Gill, ever the romantic, kept an eye on me if we went clubbing together and I dishonestly colluded with her maternal attentions. I don't think she could bear the idea of two women who'd made it through six years finally throwing in the towel.

Inevitably Mandy crossed my path again. Dulcie was a distant memory, my concern for her diluted by the pas-sage of time, but she catapulted back into my thoughts at a Scandles fancy dress night. I'd been really original, going as Radclyffe Hall, quite fancying myself in the black tails and red cumberband – until I went through the door and into about 50 other Hall look-alikes, some of whom would have made Radclyffe herself look femme. So I told anybody who asked that I was supposed to be Gluck, and nobody knew who I was talking about.

Mandy was there, as a punk. I thought she probably didn't remember me, or couldn't see through my disguise, but a couple of hours into the evening she appeared at my elbow. The noise was deafening and I couldn't catch everything she said, but what it amounted to was her gratitude for getting her home that night at Mira's – what a slag *she* was! – and did I fancy a pull of her joint? Just to be sociable I accepted and in return poured her a plastic cupful of Hock. After that there didn't seem much to say so I asked her how she was getting on at the Sea Chalet.

'I'm out of there, thank Christ,' she shouted. Then I think she said something about it being 'a bad scene'.

'How's Mr Prince – Sidney?'

'What?'

I repeated the question and she looked at me as though I was daft. 'He's dead,' she said.

I mouthed something about it being awful, poor old chap, and when did it happen?

She took a drag of her joint and moved closer. 'Promise you won't tell no one?' I nodded. 'They did it, the bastards, the same time as Dulcie. You won't tell no one?' Her eyes were black-lined blots of anxiety. 'Promise?'

I promised, but I didn't understand what she was telling me. 'I saw him,' I shouted, putting my head right next to her's. 'That day I visited. He was alive then.' Almost. I heard again phlegmy purr.

Mandy wanted to go, but I held onto her arm. 'He wasn't dead when I visited.'

She scanned the room as if looking for an escape.

'If he was dead,' I persisted, 'who –'

'It wasn't Sidney. They couldn't risk you – I shouldn't have told you.'

'Why couldn't risk what?' I tightened my grip on her arm.

'Get off,' she growled, jerking herself free. 'None of your business anyway. What's it to you?'

She shot off into the crowd and I stood for several seconds, aware that people were looking. But it was *my* business: they – Catterell – had lied to me. Why go to all the bother of showing me a sick old man if Sidney was already dead? I thought of the awful room in semi-darkness, the smell of waiting death, the teeth in the water on the bedside table – where I'd left the envelope. The envelope that Catterell had offered to take from me on the steps of the hostel; had telephoned to suggest I 'pop' in the post. And when that didn't work had substituted another of his residents for Sidney, a dying man who obviously didn't understand what was going on. But Mandy had known what was going on. Had been in on it. Why tell me now?

I looked round the room and spotted her among a group of Golden Girls. I threaded through the dancers.

'Mandy, I have to talk to you,' I told her.

Even with the mind-numbing decibel level of the music her voice came through loud and clear: 'FUCK OFF! LEAVE ME ALONE!'

Fighting my horror of public scenes I tried again: 'Look, it's important. You can't just leave it at that.'

Heads were turning as people sensed the prelude to a lovers' tiff or a cat fight between rivals. Some sensible souls started to put space between themselves and the shit they thought was about to fly; others stayed put, at the ringside.

I lowered my voice, hoping Mandy wouldn't feel so threatened. 'I don't want to involve you,' I began. 'I just want to –'

I saw the Doc Martin start its swing long before it made contact with my shin, but I never even glimpsed the be-ringed fist that sunk between my jaw and my cheekbone. Through watering eyes I tried to anticipate where the next blow was coming from, but Mandy managed to get in a couple more kicks and punches before a Dolly Parton with a drooping moustache got her in a full-Nelson. She was still lashing out and screaming obscenities when they dragged her into a corner and made calm-down noises. I was too stunned to move and just stood there, staring at her.

'Come on now,' said a big man who looked like a Spitting Image version of Shirley Bassey, even down to the cleavage, 'all over now.' He put his hands firmly but gently on my shoulders and turned me round so I was facing away from Mandy. 'Just go back to your friends. We don't want any trouble – it's Christmas.'

Gill, Maureen and Ellie shepherded me back to our

table and I went like a lamb. I wanted to have a really good cry but was aware that the spectators were still hanging about for the denouement, the one they knew and loved so well. They'd have to wait a long time, I thought, gritting my teeth – my teeth! Ellie was dabbing at my mouth with a handful of tissues while Gill was casting dark and dangerous looks towards Mandy's corner. Something hard was rolling around inside my mouth. I held a hand under my chin and spat. One of the few teeth that hadn't yet been filled hit my palm in a spray of blood.

'Is there a tooth fairy in the house?' I asked. Ellie started to giggle and Maureen caught it. Tension splintered into nervous laughter and we were clutching one another like a bunch of dopey schoolkids, the tears trickling down our creased faces.

'I don't see anything to laugh about,' Gill muttered, still glowering across the dancefloor. 'Good riddance.'

I looked up to see Mandy leaving with a couple of men, and I didn't know whether to feel relieved or frustrated: she'd dropped a bombshell, and not just on my face.

Cockburn

I lied to Jack about the bruising, telling him I'd fallen down the steps of a house after a party.

'Drunk again,' he sighed with mock exasperation.

I re-read Dulcie's notes but apart from Page 33 there weren't any further references to MI5 or the Pope. Nor could I discover what the 'women with women' bit meant because despite going through all the spare photocopies I couldn't find Page 32. If it was among the original notes I'd never know – Catterell wasn't likely to let me have them back, not if they related in any way to something he wanted kept quiet. What had Mandy said? 'They did it, the bastards, the same time as Dulcie.' Catterell killed Sidney? – it couldn't mean that. Catterell might be a slimy toad whose business dealings hadn't been all they should, but that didn't make him a murderer. If it did, then half the businessmen of England (into whose tender care Thatcher and Major had consigned the country) were indictable.

I went through Page 33 again. Dulcie's parish priest would know a lot about her, but it was out of the question going to him. For one thing, whatever she told him would be confidential, and for another, I imagined he'd had as much trouble making head or tail of her disjointed mind as I had. I could go to the police, but my experience as a court reporter had taught me that the police weren't interested in the ravings of an ex-psychiatric patient. They'd give about the same credence to a teenage heroine addict, even if they could find her. I didn't know where she lived – but I knew a woman who did. I dialled Bill Fletcher's number and asked to speak to Mandy's PO.

'Sorry, can't help you,' she said. 'Mandy's probation has finished and I haven't seen her since. She's not obliged to keep in touch.'

'Can you give me her address?'

'I can, but there's no guarantee she'll still be there. She used to move around quite a lot. Hang on – Alec! D'you know if Mandy's still on the estate? Thanks – and put the lamp down, there's a good lad. No luck I'm afraid. You could try the Sea Chalet.'

'I think she's left there.'

'That's news to me. I wonder where she's getting her money from. I happen to know she's back on the needle and it doesn't come cheap.' The PO sighed. Hers was a thankless task sometimes. 'She's probably on the game.'

Alec started messing around with the lamp again, so she excused herself in order to kill him. 'If you find out where she is you might let us know. I'll try and get the Drug Centre to counsel her.' She didn't sound too hopeful about that. I went through the notes again. Dr Cockburn – was that Dulcie's joke? Nobody was listed under that name in the phone book, but then if he was a a psychiatrist he wouldn't be in the directory, would he? You twit! If he was treating Dulcie he'd probably be known to Mrs D. I rang her.

'No, never heard of that one. Dulcie's doctor was Mrs Varley, a lovely woman, a medical doctor, you know.'

'But was she under a psychiatrist?' I persisted.

'Don't know,' said Mrs D. 'The place she used to be at shut – that's why she came here. And anyway, they don't make house calls. Mrs Varley would know.'

'Is she local?'

'Just round the corner – why?'

I couldn't think up a good enough reason. 'I just wanted to talk to her,' I said.

'They don't discuss their patients with any old body,' said Mrs D. meaning that *she* wasn't to be classed in that category.

Dr Varley's receptionist was the protective, nosy type: 'What's it about?' I told her it was private and she countered by asking if I was a patient.

'No, it's personal.'

She sniffed. 'Doctor's very busy right now. You'll have to wait until the end of surgery – and then she's got house calls to make, so you'll have to be quick.'

I rang back just before noon, fully expecting Varley to give me the cold shoulder, so I did a bit of ingratiating, apologising for taking up her time, and told her who I was and how I'd known Dulcie.

'Of course! My sister-in-law used to attend one of your classes – it was me who suggested that Dulcie take up writing. Sorry about that – it didn't work out?'

'That's partly it,' I admitted. 'I felt awful when I heard about her death.'

'Don't give it another thought,' said Varley. 'You weren't in any way to blame. In fact, I don't know what made her do it – she wasn't the suicidal type. She was far too angry. Plucky, too. Her mission in life was to take on the psychiatric establishment – she had a real bee in her bonnet about that, as I'm sure you discovered.'

Encouraged by her friendliness I said 'Could I ask you something?'

'Depends what it is.'

'Did she seemed depressed at the time? Was she on tranquillizers or anything like that?'

'Ah, now I *can* talk about that because it was made

50

public at the inquest – didn't you read the paper report?'

I hadn't.

'Don't blame you,' said Varley. 'Gruesome things. Anyway, I hadn't prescribed any medication for Dulcie for several weeks because she was so much more in control. Oh she blathered on sometimes about religion and sex, but if we tranquillized people for denouncing MI5 and talking dirty, two thirds of the population would be comatose – *I'd* be comatose.'

I wondered whether Dulcie could have got hold of drugs elsewhere – 'on the street?'

'Now why would she want to do that? She hated taking anything – thought it was a plot by MI5.'

'But supposing . . . '

'Supposing she had – and I can't think why she should – we'd be none the wiser anyway. Somehow or other, and it doesn't bear thinking about, she managed to pour half a bottle of bleach down her throat. There's not an awful lot left for a pathologist to analyse after that. If I were you'd I'd forget poor Dulcie. Whatever possessed her to do what she did is a mystery we'll never understand. She was getting on so well, but you have to remember that she had a long history of mental disturbance – anything could have plunged her back, but it certainly wasn't your class. She told me she left because she hadn't got time with her marriage coming up.'

'Did you believe that?'

Varley chuckled. 'About the marriage, you mean? Yes, and no: Dulcie thought she was getting married, and that made her happy.'

'Did you know her boyfriend, Mr Prince?'

'Nice old boy,' said the doctor.'I met him at the hostel when he came courting Dulcie. Mind you, he must have been at least 20 years older than her, but he never contradicted her when she rattled on about the wedding. Never confirmed it either.'

'Did you know he died?' I asked.

Varley was surprised. 'He seemed fit enough, if a little vague. Of course, he'd have had his own doctor.'

No, Sidney was not at Dulcie's inquest, Dulcie hadn't been receiving psychiatric treatment for some time, and

Varley hadn't heard of a Dr Cockburn – and . . . she was sorry but she had a call in ten minutes and had to fly. I thanked her and hung up.

I sat for a bit, tonguing the hole where my tooth should have been and wondering if my overdraft would stretch to a session with the dentist. There didn't seem much point – he could hardly put it back again. And I couldn't bring Dulcie back either. What had Varley said? 'She wasn't the suicidal type – she was far too angry.'

Had somebody been angry with her? – angry enough to waylay her just out of sight of a busy shopping area and –

I snatched up the phone and clamped it unthinkingly to my head, wincing. Mrs D was not amused: 'You again! I can't keep running to the phone every five minutes. What is it this time?'

I suddenly realised that I couldn't ask her if she knew Sidney was dead: if she was in on it (whatever *it* was) she'd know somebody had told, and it wouldn't take much guessing to guess who. No wonder Mandy wanted me to stop questioning her – she knew how 'they' dealt with troublemakers.

'I thought I might pop over and see Mr Prince, it being Christmas and all,' I told Mrs D. 'But I didn't want to put my foot in it – he does know about Dulcie by now?'

Mrs D's voice softened slightly: 'Didn't you know dear? The poor old thing passed on. Now let me see, it must have been soon after you called here. When was that? I remember Mr Catterell rang up to tell us and he said it was a shame Sidney couldn't have hung on for the Guy Fawkes party – they put on a lovely show for their guests, and Sidney was looking forward to the fireworks. Love him.'

I was no better informed than before, and I couldn't really see Mrs D as a Jekyll and Hyde character. Catterell maybe, but Mrs D? . . .

I had a lot of thinking to do, so I took Daisy out to the bird reserve. It was bitterly cold and blowing a gale, so I locked myself into my hooded coat and my thoughts, the binoculars still in their case. I didn't want any distractions, like spotting a rare American lesser-crested whatsit blown

3,000 miles off-course. That's where I was, off-course. I had to get my head round this one.

Dulcie died in mid-October. I tried to remember the date on Sidney's letter saying he'd saved enough for them to get married. Unless he'd suddenly changed his mind, what reason would there have been for her to kill herself? I cursed myself for meekly handing over the envelope to Catterell. Sidney died, according to Mandy, 'the same time as Dulcie', yet Catterell apparently told Mrs D he'd died near November 5th. There had to be a death certificate.

My mashed jaw was beginning to ache in sympathy with a bruised shin and I whistled Daisy to head back for the car. After I'd dropped her off at home I went over to the newspaper office and asked to see the most recent back copies. Sidney Edward Prince, aged 72, had passed away on November 3rd and would be sadly missed by all at The Sea Chalet. Why had they pretended he was still alive? If he'd been murdered and there were signs of violence on the body they'd have problems explaining them away. They'd have to wait ... until ... another body could be substituted, a body without bruises or whatever. Sidney's own doctor wouldn't necessarily see the body; it could have gone straight to the pathologist who wouldn't know Sidney from Adam – or the old boy who'd unwittingly stood in for Sidney.

I asked if Dorothy was in editorial and could spare me a few minutes.

'You still chasing Catterell?' she asked, keeping her voice down so that the front-office staff couldn't hear.

'Sort of. I know it's a cheek, but do you think you could find out which doctor's practice covers the Chalet?'

Dorothy said she'd ring me when she had anything.

She was quick, too. I hadn't been home ten minutes before she rang to tell me that the hostel was in the area served by Drs Anthony Kay, Marissa Palphramand, and Ravi Dakush. Dorothy knew Marissa – they were both opera buffs and sometimes spent holidays at Glyndebourne or The Maltings. It was Marissa whose patients included rsidents of the Chalet.

'No Dr Cockburn?' I asked without much hope.

'Cockburn?' said Dorothy. 'Now that rings bells. Wasn't

he that surgeon who was struck off? I'm talking about maybe 20 years ago. Something to do with paedophilia . . . I know! It was a child porn racket, while these things were quite rare: I mean, not talked about. It wasn't just in this country – there was a whole network across Europe. He lived in Kingston but the nationals found out he had a sister living here and asked us to see her. She was very respectable – Ladies Circle, Twinning Association, all that sort of thing. She denounced him, but she couldn't deny the fact that he'd got some of his contacts through the Association. He used to accompany her on some of the trips to the Continent and while she thought she was building international goodwill, her brother was doing a bit of entente cordiale of his own.'

'She didn't know what was going on then?'

'Nobody did. I felt quite sorry for her,' said Dorothy. 'She was one of those people for whom respectability, the public persona, is all important. Take that away and there's not much left.'

'What happened to him?'

Dorothy remembered that Cockburn had been sent down – 'But it was a long time ago, he's probably out by now. There were all sorts of men involved with him: social workers, a clergyman, businessmen . . . What's this got to do with the Sea Chalet?'

I admitted I didn't know. At this rate I'd be spending my entire waking hours out at the reserve trying to figure out what the hell was going on. I thanked Dorothy for her time, relieved that she wasn't interested professionally: you get like that after years in the business. A 'good story' that you'd have been hungry for as a youngster becomes a bind. It can mean nights sitting in a car outside somebody's house, waiting for them to put out the milk bottles so that you can leap out and have the front door slammed in your face. It means being threatened sometimes, or having dogs set on you, or Fleet Street harrassing you from the insular comfort of a warm office: 'Brighton's in your area isn't it? Pop over and see if . . . ' when Brighton's 80 miles away, it's Saturday night and you're dressed up to the nines, halfway out the door; or you're looking forward to a night in. It means all that and finding next day that your story's been spiked or reduced to one par after you've been out half the night freezing your fanny off, and spent half-an-hour dictating to a copytaker who, if you're unlucky, is either half-deaf or thinks he's a sub. I was glad to be out of the business. It was all being run by accountants, anyway, and what they knew about journalism you could poke up a beetle's bum.

The inevitability of Christmas

I faffed about in the kitchen, getting Jack's tea ready and snacking on bits from the fridge. I'd finally succumbed to the inevitability of Christmas, and the worktop was cluttered with biscuits and fruit and dog food. I wished, for the millionth time, that I was tidier, that my mind was more disciplined. Every now and then – and this was now – I saw the house for what it was: a mess that needed a good clean and a skip for the junk. My 'study' stank of Daisy's canker, the cupboard under the stairs was a rats' paradise of old evil-smelling trainers and damp outdoor clothing; the Ali Baba in the bathroom was bulging with unwashed undies, and the kitchen would have been condemned if it was in a restaurant. On top of my raised consciousness about my slum, I'd bored my girlfriend into the arms of the law, lost a class worth £32 a week, had a tooth forcibly extracted, and Christmas was coming up on me like a road-hog up an exhaust. I had enough trouble in mind without tossing about in Dulcie's wake.

Jack came in and sneaked up the stairs with a bulging carrier bag, but not before I spied a roll of wrapping paper sticking out. Somehow he'd saved enough cash to go Christmas shopping. While he was in his room I scribbled a note telling him his tea was ready and that I'd gone shopping.

There was a queue at the cash dispenser, which provided me with a good excuse not to get an account balance. Armed with my plastic money I launched myself into the unfestive shoppers. It was getting towards closing time and there weren't that many people about to get in the way, but I took ages choosing what I wanted. I went into Young Man with the idea of buying Jack a flash winter jacket. The shop was a plastic and steel tubes job on several unnecessary levels that would have made it difficult for many disabled people. Most of the staff looked about 15 and displayed all the attentiveness of dead tortoises. Nobody asked if I wanted help as I sorted through the racks, peering through my glasses at the price tags, and wincing. I could have helped myself to anything and at those prices it would have served them right. I dismissed a nasty little thought about Jack helping himself, preferring to fantasise that he'd been uncharacteristically careful with his pocket money, or even that he'd been winning at the arcade I'd asked him not to frequent.

As I flicked away another price tag in disgust I became aware that I was being trailed by an assistant who, when I looked up, pretended to be tidying the ties or boxer shorts. After a few minutes of hide and seek I sidled up to him: 'Can I help you?' I asked.

The few areas of umpimpled skin on his face flushed pink. I couldn't hear what he said over the cochlea-crunching din of musak and I inclined my head towards him. He oozed Brute and his shirt sleeves were too short.

' . . . and we've been told to be vigilant,' he was saying, importantly and awkwardly.

I gathered he was referring to shoplifting. 'Do I look like a shoplifter?' I asked him.

He got a bit snotty: 'We can't be too careful.'

'Or too helpful.'

He didn't know what to say next, a desire to revert to playground language warring with his new status as a responsible member of the Young Man sales team.

I sighed. 'Perhaps you can help me choose a jacket for a 15 year old. You'll have a better idea – and you can make sure I don't stuff a duffel coat up my knicker leg.'

He was okay after that and surprisingly knowledgeable and useful. We parted the best of friends, me clutching an oversized carrier bag containing a leather and green denim coat that had cost me £20 more than I'd intended.

I'd just time to get a tree that didn't look as if it'd been grown in a straight-jacket, some cheap wrapping paper off one of the frozen street vendors, and three packs of charity greeting cards. I found myself looking for something for Sue before I remembered that we wouldn't be doing that this year, and experienced a tug of sadness. We never spent Christmas together anyway because she had family in Purley who thought lesbian women were on a par with pubic lice. I didn't blame her for not telling them about our relationship: there's enough oppression in the world without being disowned by your nearest and dearest. And they were dear to her – nice 'normal' people who thought the world was a terrible place in which the 2.2 family, the Queen and that nice Mr Major were the last bastions of decency in a tide of violence, sex and drugs that they read about avidly every day. They believed in the sanctity of life so were anti-abortion and pro-capital punishment, thought all gays ought to be gassed, tut-tutted when the National Front invaded the terraces, and sincerely believed that all this racism stuff didn't exist until lefties started getting blacks excited over nothing.

I supposed Sue would pass off her policewoman as 'my friend', as she had done with me until I refused to visit Purley ever again: all that separate bedrooms and no kissing under the mistletoe . . .

It would be just me and Jack again.

Real families

As it turned out, it was just me. Jack hung around long enough on Christmas morning to scoff chocolates for breakfast and then went off in his new jacket to meet his mates, promising to come back for dinner. That was the last I saw of him until the evening when he came in smothered in shaving cream and reeking of canned lager.

'Hi my little old mum.' His voice had the sing-song quality of the slightly sloshed and his eyeballs weren't in sync. He crushed me in a bear hug and started to chant 'Jingle Bells'.

'I think you'd better go to bed,' I told him. 'I gave your dinner to the dog anyway.'

'S'alright mum – I ate at Danny's.'

They'd had chicken nuggets and burgers. I thought of the time I'd spent roasting duck in black cherry sauce and brandy.

'Anyway I'm not tired. What's on telly?'

Jack switched on the box and flopped in front of it. Within minutes he was asleep. I sent the inane television revellers back into the ether and resumed my book, determined not to be hurt. After all, what 15 year old wants to spend Christmas with his mother? I twiddled my toes in the monstrous pair of tiger feet slippers Jack had given me and which I kept tripping up in. The fairy lights on the tree blurred and I rubbed my eyes fiercely. Come on, there's a lot worse off than you. I poured myself another Benedictine, stoked up the fire, and escaped into Marge Piercy's Utopian world of 'Woman on the Edge of Time'.

I expected Jack to have a hangover the next morning: even wished it on him using that curious parental logic that insists he'd be learning a salutory lesson. But he dragged himself off the livingroom floor at an almost respectable hour, stoked himself up on a massive cooked breakfast and half a box of Quality Street and then prepared himself for an arduous session watching more telly. I reminded him that we were doing the usual Boxing Day ramble with friends, but he declined, offering to do the washing up and to vacuum the carpet if I let him off.

'You can go mum – do your hangover good, a good walk.'

I protested, not entire truthfully, that I'd been very abstemious the day before.

'Oh yeah, I can see,' he said, pointing to the half-full bottle of Benedictine.

'You know, it was never meant to be like this,' I told him. 'When I was expecting you I had all these idiot dreams about having a child who'd like the things I like – bird-watching and rambling and . . . all that.'

'Never mind, mum,' he said brightly, 'at least you've got me.'

The women arrived in Gill's rusty old Volvo and for some time the house was full of kids and dogs and chocolate wrappers. Jack played mock fights with the younger ones and almost capitulated to their demands that he come on the walk, but a phone call from one of his mates saved him.

'Have a good time,' he said as I left, juggling with walking boots, binoculars, rucksack and Daisy.

The day was cold and overcast, but we did have a good time – one of the last for quite a while. Gill drove us out to the South Downs and we trekked up a footpath through empty fields to one of the best views in the county. After a brief collapse for hot coffee and fags we headed into the woods, stuffing our pockets with sweet chestnuts and fir cones, and frightening pheasants from cover. By the time we reached the halfway mark (which just happened to be a pub) we were flushed by the cold wind and a sense of freedom. We scattered ourselves over the greasy black flagstones as near to the fire as we could and went through the menu which consisted mainly of black pudding doorsteps, bacon doorsteps, cheese and onion doorsteps and, as a concession to vegetarians, lentil doorsteps.

On the way back to the car, along a different route, I fell back and watched my friends and their children. They weren't 'real' families, of course; they didn't fit the homophobic fantasy ideal. There was Maureen who had escaped her husband after years of abuse. Ellie was piggy-backing Rachel's seven-year-old son up and down a grassy slope: he was a bright child, one of those children who ask unanswerable questions and don't whine in supermarkets. Rachel'd had him courtesy of a gay friend, and she and Rufus were a happy enough pair. Gill's teenage daughter Minny was walking beside her mother, talking in her calm quiet way. Gill and her husband had split when Minny was 12. He'd got involved with a younger woman and Gill's family said it was her fault because she was a lesbian. But Ed had been screwing around for years.

Now Gill was with Rachel, Ellie was between men, and
Maureen was enjoying her freedom with her children. It
would be a long time before she trusted anyone enough
to share her life with them.

I stopped to spy on a knot of red-legged partridge for-
aging in a derelict barn.

'What is it?' Maureen had been even further back and
now caught up with me.

I gave her the binoculars and watched her as she
watched the fat stripey birds. She had almost translucent
skin stretched tightly over small, fine bones. I wondered
if it was her apparent vulnerability that attracted men to
her; had made one of them want to smash her face in.
Did it begin with an urge to protect? – or to own? And
where did the original intention – to love and honour –
become perverted into anger that could explode into the
violence of torture? I thought of all the women who'd
told their stories in the writing classes; their poems and
short stories a seemingly never-ending flow of subtle
oppression by men who, consciously or not, whittled
down their confidence and sense of self. The 'gentlemen'
who treated them like invalids or infants until they no
longer felt competent enough to choose their own library
books or clothes, couldn't make a decision any more
demanding than whether to buy butter or margarine.

'Penny for them,' said Maureen, linking her arm
through mine.

'Why do women feel guilty?'

We plodded along in the dying afternoon, the
children's voices ringing back to us in the clear cold air.

Unpremeditated sex

I asked her again that night as we lay in front of the fire,
the light dancing along our bodies. What had happened
hadn't been intentional, at least not premeditated. Gill,
Rachel and Ellie had gone home. Maureen's two had
snuggled down with Jack to watch tv in his room, and

60

when it came time to go we'd found all three warm and deep-breathing in his bed, their sleeping faces lit by the flickering screen. In whispers we'd agreed not to disturb them and returned to the livingroom to talk. But there hadn't been any talking. As if we both knew we'd put our arms round one another. Touching became kissing; kissing a kind of hunger. She slowed me and I was stunned by her power, the strength of her self-assurance.

Now we lay side by side, heads propped on hands. I smoothed the line of her hip where it caught the fire's glow.

'Why do women feel guilty?'

She looked at me in surprise. 'Do you?'

'About this? No.' I leant forward and touched her collar bones with my mouth. The hollow between the bone and her neck was slightly damp, tasting of warm skin and salt. 'I meant women generally: that irrational guilt about something that isn't your fault.'

She sat up, pulling her knees in so that she could rest her chin on them. 'I used to feel guilty. When he hit me I thought it was my fault. When he raped me I thought that in some way I'd made him do it. He liked me to wear short skirts – you know, the clinging kind, and heels that were too high. He wanted me to look like a tart, but when other men looked he accused me of encouraging them. And you know what?' – she turned her head so that she looked at me – 'I believed him. I got so screwed up trying to be what he wanted me to be. Trouble was, he didn't know what he wanted me to be.'

I wanted to hug her but her silence was so total, she seemed to have withdrawn into a deep, unreachable part of herself. The fire was dying and shadows gathered like bruises on her body. Carefully I pulled open the draught control in the hearth and worked a couple of logs into the embers. The silence stretched between us. I'd never been where she had been and couldn't be where she was now.

And then she said 'He was confused.'

I felt a surge of my own anger at her tolerance, and somehow she picked it up: 'It isn't an excuse, it's a reason – there have to be reasons.' Maureen leant over and touched my arm. 'He used to bring these magazines home and leave them lying around so that I'd see them. He hated the women in the pictures. He used to say there were only two kinds of women – the ones you fucked and the ones you married.' She caught my look. 'But you see, to him it was a compliment.'

I couldn't keep the cynicism out of my voice when I asked her where it went wrong. She thought for a while, as she must have been thinking for years, trying to recognise the stages in their relationship so that she could make sense of what seemed to be senselessness

She shook her head, reached out for her drink. 'I don't know. It's like being married to several men instead of just the one – I don't understand – can't – he didn't either. Forget it.'

I moved over to her. I wanted to say 'It's all over now' but it wasn't, not for Maureen and all the women it had happened to, and all the women it was waiting for.

Resolutions

There were still a couple of weeks before the start of the new term and I made a resolution on the eve of the New Year to put the old one behind me, and not take on board my students' personal problems. Since Boxing Day I hadn't seen Maureen in any other situation than that of a friend in the group, and knew it would never be otherwise. Neither of us would let ourselves be drawn into a romantic relationship and it wasn't necessary to contrive another sexual encounter. If it happened, it would.

If at night Sue intruded on my thoughts I banished her with the lists. I'd filled in J, K, L, M and N, but that wasn't entirely due to Sue. Exorcising Dulcie, Sidney and Mandy wasn't easy, but I couldn't figure it all out and I didn't feel like harrassing myself any more. So somebody did it for me.

It was a stupid thing to do, I know, but when Sue and three other women, who included Pc Plod, turned up at Scandles that night, I decided the place wasn't big enough for all of us. If Sue saw me she wasn't going to let it show. And if her apparent happiness was contrived it didn't make it any easier. She had a marvellous smile involving her teeth which were like the ones you see in dental adverts on television; and the smile included her eyes so that they seemed to be lighting up exclusively for whoever she was looking at, which that night wasn't me. I didn't want to see her eyes doing that for someone else. It was too soon. I didn't want to think of her at all, but you can't just erase some memories overnight. You try not to remember intimate details but they stick to you, and then you're wondering if those same things are being said and done with somebody else. Once you're on that treadmill the next step is wondering whether there are different things being said and done and, if so, why hadn't they been said and done with you? Then, if you're sensible, you get tired of such mental convolutions and find yourself somebody else or hibernate before you end up throwing wobblies in the women's loo.

Maureen was there that night and I could have put on my own show of indifference to Sue, but it would have been a cheap deception and Maureen was worth more than that. So I left.

Gill was exasperated: 'Why do you both have to let it make such a difference?' she demanded as we stood outside on the steps of the club. She meant, couldn't we part without creating a schism in the group? 'You're behaving like a couple of heterosexuals – it's ludicrous!'

'Just because we're women –'

'And feminists, so-called – '

'Alright,' I sighed, 'but you're letting ideology get the better of you.'

She looked as if I'd punched her on the nose.

'For god's sake, Gill, this is reality. The problems are the same whatever relationship you're in. The problems are the same.'

'They shouldn't be,' she called after me as I walked off along the seafront, thinking I could find a taxi. Instead I found trouble.

Night life

The seafront is a long stretch of tatty arcades and pubs, chip shops and cafes. They were all shut but there were a couple of nightclubs that pulled in late trade and spilled it back onto the prom when it was full of booze and looking for someone to pick on or somewhere to puke. Police cars patrolled the area, but there wasn't one in sight that night.

There wasn't a taxi at the rank either so I went looking for a phone. When I saw the knot of men on the other side of the vandalised box I chickened out and decided to go back to Scandles to call a taxi from there, but in the time it took me to make the decision I'd slowed down, stopped, dithered, and tried to look casual before I made a U-turn. There'd been the usual animated conversation you expect from men on the street after midnight – over-loud out-of-context Chaucerian repartee – but when they noticed me it all went quiet. I cursed myself for getting into a situation and tried to remember anything from the self-defence class. 'When on the street act as if you belong . . .'

'Hello darling.'

While I was wrestling with my body language, a couple of yobboes had detached themselves from the group and were sauntering towards me. 'What we got here then?'

We'd got somebody who badly wanted to run. But – Stage 2 was 'Never run'.

One of them slung an arm round my shoulder and I sidestepped like a scolded cat. Stage 3 – 'Do not show fear'.

'What's the matter darling – nervous?' He looked not a lot older than Jack but a lot meaner. 'Come on – give us a smile, we're not going to hurt you.'

I felt in my pocket for my keys and made a fist around them so that they stuck out like spikes between my fingers; if anybody was going to get a faceful I hoped it was the pock-marked leering yob circling me as if I was a dangerous animal. The other one joined in and they were like dogs baiting a bear, enjoying my humiliation and, even more, my fear. But anger was beginning to leak into the fear like acid in blood.

'You bloody cowards!' My voice was reedy and high-pitched, just when I wanted it to be deep and intimidating.

'Ooh, posh are we?' The one with the Gruyere skin laughed at his own joke and feinted at me like a boxer several times, his tattooed knuckles flicking out and making me blink involuntarily. Then he was close enough: the toe of my shoe sunk into his crutch hard enough to imprint the stitching of his greasy jeans on his pubic bone. As he doubled over I leant on his head with one hand intending to ram his face into my upcoming knee, but a hand grabbed my arm and I was swung round to find the other yob screaming 'Fucking old cow!' into my face. I didn't get him full with the keys but they gouged the side of his jaw as they scraped by.

'Oih! Pack it in.'

A big body shoved between us and I was flailing about trying to land one on it, anywhere. 'Bloody hell, miss – you're a little goer!'

As my eyes began to focus again I saw Danny, holding me easily at arms length.

'I'd hate to see you when you was angry, miss,' he said, grinning hugely. 'Where'd you learn to bollock a bloke like that?' Danny turned to look unsympathetically at my victim. 'Serves you right Baz – you always were a twat. This is my teacher – she's not the filth, you dozy bastard.' He had a way with words, did Danny. 'They thought you was the filth and we were doing a bit of business – know what I mean?'

I knew what he meant.

The rest of his group had gathered round, curious no doubt about the 'little tit'.

'She's my writing tutor,' said Danny with a touch of pride. 'Helping me write my memoirs, aren't you miss?' Some of the men laughed, but it was deferential: they obviously didn't mess with Danny.

'I was looking for a taxi,' I said, inanely. My legs were doing their wet string impersonation and my teeth were clicking against one another.

65

'Ricki, go and get a taxi for miss.' Danny put an arm round me. 'You oughtn't be round here at night, it's not a nice place for a lady.'

I laughed weakly. 'Nice of you to say so Danny, but I'm not a lady.'

'No, straight up, miss – the only women round here are tarts – or dogs like her.' He indicated someone in the group and for the first time I noticed Mandy, that white face stark against the black leather and blue denim of the men. I supposed she was there for business purposes, plying her trade or buying, I didn't know or care. I'd only just got over the bruises she'd inflicted and I could sense fresh ones beginning to bloom where I'd been grabbed.

Ricki shouted from the phone box 'Half-hour wait.'

'Don't bother,' Danny told him. 'We'll get her home. Where d'you live, miss?' I told him and looked round for his car. 'Don't worry about that – there's plenty of wheels about. Ricki – go and hot-wire something. No crap, get something juicy.'

I started to protest, but Danny wouldn't hear of it: they'd only be borrowing the motor. They did it all the time. 'Hey-up – here he comes.'

A BMW roared up to the kerb, the doors swinging open before it had stopped. Two men slithered out of the front seats and somebody screamed 'It's the filth!' and I was being swept along the pavement by Danny. We got as far as the multi-storey car park before we realised we weren't being chased. As one we turned, ready to bolt round the corner.

'What the fuck? – they got Mandy!'

'So what? Let 'em have the slag.'

'Hang about,' said Danny, 'that's not the regular filth. What's going on?'

One of the men was repeatedly slamming Mandy against the metal shutters of a souvenir shop. He had a good grip on her spiky hair and intermittently slapped her about, yelling 'What've you done with them?' while the other man was trying to search her.

Danny started walking back. 'You looking for me?' he shouted.

The rest of his group stayed put and I could foresee

Danny getting into big trouble. While we'd waited for Ricki to return I'd seen the little packets changing hands and watched Danny stuff the unsold ones into his pockets. I ran up behind him and hissed 'They'll find the stuff on you' but he wasn't listening.

'You're big brave blokes when it comes to a tart – how'd you fancy taking on me instead?'

The man knocking Mandy about carried on as if nothing had happened, but the other one took time off from searching her to look up, spit 'Piss off' and return to his work.

For a heavy person Danny was quick. He hauled the smaller one off Mandy and pulled him straight into a head-butt before dropping him like a rag doll to the pavement. The taller man, still holding onto Mandy's hair, turned straight into the edge of Danny's hand. His nose broke and blood snaked out of both nostrils.

'Don't you want to have a go, miss?' Danny asked, grinning at me. Then he kicked the tall one's kneecap.

All I wanted was to get out of there. I grabbed Mandy and we hared back to the group with Danny behind us. He was laughing and punching the air as if he'd just scored a goal. My wet strings were back but I felt a surge of exhilaration. I hadn't done anything that exciting since ringing the fire station alarm when I was 11.

It was infectious. The whole bunch of them were whooping and cavorting, pushing and thumping one another, running mad like a pack of thug monkeys through the car park, banging on the car roofs, their cries echoing off the concrete levels. Only Mandy seemed unaffected, slopping along behind me, her Doc Martens scraping the ground, her hands shaking as she tried to roll a cigarette. She froze like a frightened rabbit when the headlights of a car stabbed the gloom, silencing the group. An engine screamed into life and the car shot out in front of us, its tyres squealing.

My future flashed in front of my eyes: TEACHER NETTED IN DRUG SWOOP – 'MISS' IS GANGSTER'S MOLL –

'Ricki, my man! Where've you been you little git?'

Ricki's maniacal face peered over the top of the driver's door: 'Sorry Dan – they was all locked except this one.'

Middle-class inhibition was reasserting itself over the adrenaline and I was becoming conscious of myself as a wrinkled alien among wild children. With the exception of Mandy they were still fired up and ready for the next high, anything to allay the boredom of the seaside town in winter or life in general. I finally convinced Danny I wasn't riding in any stolen car, not because I thought it was wrong, which I did, but because I couldn't rid myself of a horror of getting caught. Worse, getting caught by Pc Plod.

Ricki was revving the engine and the others were calling to Danny to get in. I could see he was torn between what he wanted to do and what he thought he ought to. 'Go on Danny – don't worry about me. I'll get a taxi from the railway station. It's not far.'

He hesitated, looking at me and then at the overcrowded white Sierra.

'Nah,' he said at last. 'I'll walk you there. Those scumbags might be looking for us.' He suddenly seemed to notice Mandy again. 'I wanna talk to you. You go with us.'

The others screeched off onto the street, the stolen car heeling over as Ricki tried to avoid the iron railings on the opposite pavement. 'Mad bastard,' said Danny cheerfully.

I thought we were going to the station straight away, but Danny had other ideas.

'Alright,' he said, turning to Mandy, 'what's it all about then?' His voice was hard.

Mandy wouldn't look at him. 'Don't know what you mean,' she said.

'Don't give me that. You been buying coke like you was a fucking heiress. Where'd you get the money?' He made a swipe at her that wasn't meant to connect and she shied back glaring at him, more sulkily than in anger.

'Come on, Danny,' I protested. 'There's no need –'

'You don't understand, miss. This little cow could have set us up. How else would she've got the money?'

'How d'you think?' Mandy muttered.

Danny poked her shoulder with his finger. 'You couldn't make that much darling, don't kid yourself, state you're in . . . If you want another fix in this town – ever – you'll tell me who those two greasers were. Because,' he poked her again, hard enough to make her stumble backwards, 'they wasn't the local filth. They was either from away or – I dunno. You tell me.'

'It's got nothing to do with you,' said Mandy. Danny took a step towards her. 'I mean, it's got nothing to do with dealing. They wasn't after you so what's it matter?'

'So who were they?' Danny persisted .

'Just some blokes. I nicked something from a place I was working at.'

'What?'

Mandy's fingers twisted her jacket as if she was trying to screw up courage to tell him either to get stuffed, or the truth. He gave her a little encouragement. 'Either tell me or give me back the dope.' His hand shot out and pulled her to him. He searched her pockets and pulled out a couple of white packets.

'I paid you for them!' she screamed, trying to force them out of his hand, her fear of him overridden by her need. 'You bastard! I paid you.'

'For god's sake, Danny – give it to her,' I pleaded

He thrust a fistful of crumpled notes at her. 'Here, take it. It's the last fix you get. Come on, miss, let's get you home. She's not worth the bother.'

Mandy's scream was awful, rising from a drawn-out roar of anguish to the high note of panic. I felt self-disgust, disgust with her, disgust at the whole situation. The scream gave way to a pathetic, irritating whimpering as she ran along beside Danny, pulling at his sleeve: 'I'll tell you, I'll tell you. I got to have it.'

He didn't even slow down.

'For Christ's sake, Danny. . .' I said.

'When she tells me what I want to know.'

Mascara ran in black trickles down Mandy's face. 'It's some dirty pictures,' she sobbed. 'I took them from the place I worked.'

Danny stopped and looked at her incredulously. 'Porny postcards? They was going to do you for that? Give me a break.'

'It's true! Can I have the stuff. I told you.'

'What's so special about dirty pictures?' Danny looked at me as if I might have the answer.

'Depends who's in them,' I suggested, almost as anxious as Mandy to placate him.

'Yeah, it would wouldn't it,' he said thoughtfully. 'Why'd you nick them, Mand?'

'Can I have the stuff?' she whined.

'In a minute, when you've told me.'

'For money – what do think?'

'Not to sell?' His hand slid to his trouser pocket and then paused, tantalisingly.

Impatiently I asked 'Do you mean for blackmail, something like that?'

She shot a resentful sideways glance at me as if I had no right to get involved.

'So where are these pictures?' Danny persisted. I could see the way his mind was working: if Mandy could make money out of this, so might he.

'Give me the stuff. PLEASE!'

Danny made up his mind: 'No. You show me the pictures and then you can have it.'

She knew she was beaten. 'They're at my place.'

'Right.' Danny got a firm grip on her arm. 'That's where we're going then. First we'll get teach' to the station and then you can show me your photos – they must be red-hot if someone's willing to pay the sort of dosh you been chucking about.'

I thought longingly of my nice warm bed. 'I'm coming too,' I told Danny.

'Hang about. This isn't the sort of thing you want to get mixed up in.'

I knew it was meant as a compliment. There's women you screw and women you marry. There's ladies and whores – and Danny had the power to decide which is which. I looked at Mandy shivering in her skin-tight skirt, and then down at my trouser-clad legs and sensible shoes.

'There aren't any trains anyway,' I said

Danny blew out his cheeks in frustration. 'Bloody hell, miss – I'll get you a taxi.'

'I want to make sure she's alright,' I said. 'I know more about this than you think.'

'You don't know nothing,' Mandy snarled. She turned to Danny: 'I don't want her in on it. None of her business.'

'In that case, she better come along,' he said. 'Only don't say I didn't warn you, miss.'

An exchange of packets

Mandy's place turned out to be the basement of a derelict terrace that had been abandoned. That is to say, the local council had declared it a slum and shunted the occupants into high-rise flats rather than renovate. Some smart developer would buy it cheap, dress up the decay and make a packet selling them as des.res.

The area steps were littered with broken glass and rubbish that the wind had blown through the pavement railings. None of the street lights were working and I held on to the inside railings with their fleur-de-lis heads – until one of them crunched in its rotted concrete socket and swung out over the darkened area, and then I felt my way down along the pavement wall.

'I thought you was in that squat over by the park,' Danny said as Mandy shouldered open a weather-warped door at the bottom of the steps.

'I was but I couldn't go back there after I nicked the pictures, in case they found me.'

We followed her into blackness, Danny swearing as he slipped on brick rubble in the narrow passage. The place stank of wet rot and my groping hands found long strips of torn wallpaper and exposed lathes.

'Where's the fucking light?' Danny demanded.

Ahead of me Mandy flicked on her lighter as she turned left into a room; then Danny's bulk blocked my view of her and the flame. I followed him through, holding on to the back of his jacket.

'Get the fucking lights on,' he told her.

'I'm doing it.' There was a hiss and the purr of gas and the depressing yellow of a camping lantern illuminated

71

Mandy's home. I suppose I expected squalor, but the basement was neat, tidier than my place. Mandy had nailed some sort of material over the window, there was what looked like an almost-new carpet covering the middle of the floor, and a good quality sleeping bag on top of that. Next to a ghetto blaster on a wooden palette were two cardboard boxes, one containing groceries, the other a kettle and cups; carefully arranged on the remaining space were eye-liners, lipstick, face cream, nail varnish and a box of tampons.

'Real home from home,' Danny muttered. 'Where's the pictures?'

Mandy went to the chimney piece and stuck her arm up the flue. Then she held out a folded carrier bag. 'What about the dope?'

They exchanged packets and she darted into the next room, presumably to prepare the stuff. Or maybe she sniffed it straight, I didn't know.

Danny riffled through the photographs. 'You sure you want to see these?' He sounded embarrassed.

They were high-gloss colour prints taken, I guessed, with an expensive camera. I was glad the light in the basement was weak.

'Ask her where she got them.' My voice was not much louder than the purring lamp.

'Where'd you get these?' Danny shouted through to Mandy. I heard her reply but I don't know what she said. I just kept flipping through the photographs, trying not to take in too much detail, trying not to stamp on my memory forever the brutal images of Dulcie, her genitalia spread like raw meat for the camera's dispassionate gaze, her drug-pacified eyes staring blankly beneath the bandaged forehead.

I heard Danny say 'I don't know what all the fuss is about. They're just dirty pictures – who'd want them back? They wouldn't fetch more than a few quid, tops.'

Unreasonably I felt anger towards him. All this woman meant to him was money; the sadistic exploitation of her vulnerability amounted to nothing more than that. My jaw was trembling and I clamped my teeth together.

'Said you shouldn't have come.'

I nodded, afraid to open my mouth. It wasn't just that I wanted to spit in his face, to punish him for the cruelty – in my throat the pressure of anger was mixed with fear and bile. I smacked the pictures down on the palette and they spread out into a montage of bodies and faces.

Helplessly Danny threw up his arms and then let his hands fall to his sides with a slap. 'What d'you want me to do?' he said.

'Where'd she get them?'

'Some old bloke at the hostel gave them to her – she says. Name of Sid. For safe-keeping. But she probably nicked them. Mandy! – get in here.'

He stuck his head into the other room. 'Shit! She's done a runner. Shall I go after her?'

I shook my head but he went anyway, leaving me with a brain full of sick images and fragments of ballpoint scribble – 'save me from J.C. – hes making me into film star!!!!! – where is the soul – pawned? NO

PORND HA HA'

I shut my eyes. Somehow Sidney had got hold of the photographs. Mandy had said 'They did it, the bastards, the same time as Dulcie' meaning that 'they' had killed them both. 'They' might not include Catterell, but he was implicated. He was there, in some of the photos, wearing a white coat and not much else. No wonder he wanted Dulcie's notes; they might have contained a reference to his sideline which, I assumed, went on at the Sea Chalet. Had he murdered her because he couldn't control her mouth? And then killed Sidney because the old man had given the photos to Mandy for 'safekeeping'?

I groaned involuntarily. Only Mandy could fill in the gaps. Where was she?

When Danny came back he was alone. 'I'll find her,' he said. 'There aren't many places she can hide in a hole like this. Anyway, she'll need another fix soon and then I'll have her.' He squatted down beside the pictures. 'What about these? What d'you want to do with them?'

'This is not just about pornography,' I told him.

'I figured that.' He shuffled through the pictures again. 'Who are these wankers? It looks like a hospital with the white coats and all.' I looked away as he went more slowly through the set. 'Here, that's Mandy with the old bird!'

women with women

'Put them away, Danny.'

'Oh, yeah, right.' He looked closely at a couple more and then put them back in the carrier bag. 'I can see –'

'Danny,' I said, 'don't get involved. You're in enough trouble as it is.' I took the packet from him and stuffed it into my pocket. 'This one's for the police and from what I hear you're not their flavour of the month.'

'You're joking! I don't know who the other perves are, but one of those blokes dressed up like a quack is a copper.'

I sat down beside him. 'What sort of copper?'

'The only sort – bent. I seen him somewhere . . .'

'They can't all be bent,' I said wearily. I felt stupid and out of my depth.

'No,' he admitted, grudgingly, 'but how do you know who is and who isn't? How do you know if you took these pictures to them that they wouldn't get binned – lost, like? They turn a blind eye when it suits them. I should know. There wasn't any plods about tonight, was there, with us dealing on the street?'

I stared at him. 'I know I'm being thick, but are you saying that they were deliberately absent?'

He laughed. 'Too right. Busy somewhere else, chasing joy-riders. It'll cost me, but it's worth it.'

'But what about the two men who turned up?'

The smug grin disappeared. 'Yeah, what about them? Maybe they wasn't the filth – but I still don't like my customers being nobbled, even if they are a pain in the arse like Mandy.'

I stood up. 'I've got to find her – I need answers. Will you do me a favour? If you find her, ring me. And Danny –' I touched his arm to try and make him understand how strongly I felt – 'don't give her a hard time. She's scared and she's got nobody to turn to, except you. Two people have died because of those pictures – and she knows why.'

Police business

I was swimming in oil. The sea was made of thick, black, undulating waves that slid slowly along the black, glass-smooth wall. On the shore were smooth, round rocks coated in the stuff and lying among them was a figure which was also oil-black except for the red and gaping flesh. I swam back and forth, like a goldfish in a square bowl, looking for a way out –

The shrieking alarm of the yuppie couple's car parked beneath my bedroom window wrenched me from the dream. My neck and chest were wet under the bunched-up duvet and I pushed it down and turned on my side, groping for the clock. It was 10.45 and right on time the church at the back of the house started tolling the faithful to prayer. Not for the first time, and especially now, I wished it was me, neatly-dressed like the women who walked past my house, finding solace in the hymn book-smelling, high-vaulted house of God where the issues could be so simple. I plumped up my pillow and lay back, shutting my eyes against the sunlight spearing through the top of the curtains where a ring had dropped off; envying the good women in their pews, envying the comfort in the brightly-burnished brass lectern and the artfully-arranged purple chrysanths with their stern perfume. The male focus of their worship wouldn't choke their voices as they sung their tributes or bent their knees to pay obeisance, or scrub the cold chequered tiles, or sort the jumble and make the jams.

I pulled the duvet back around my chin as the cold air of the bedroom turned my sweat to a chilly grease. Would the good women forgive Dulcie her 'sins'? Would their god exonerate her for going to her death without confessing or receiving the last rites? At least she'd been clean inside –

Angrily I slid out of bed, out of my mind and the way it was taking me. As I pulled on a track suit a blob of warmth seeped out of my vagina. And there was that, too.

Jack was still asleep on the living-room floor where I'd

found him when I slunk home. I tucked him into his sleeping bag and smoothed his hedgehog hair, then gave Daisy a bigger-than-usual breakfast and promised her a proper walk. An iron claw was scraping the insides of my uterus. Mentally I cringed as I remembered the boozy, mindless music, and the satisfaction of burying my foot in a man's crutch; the exhilaration of the neon night; the poverty of Mandy's existence and the expensive gloss of the photographs.

In the shower I tried to wash it all away with scalding water. Two Anadins and a pint of tea later I accepted it.

It was low tide so for a change I took Daisy to the beach on the opposite side of town to the reserve. I used to enjoy walking her there because she liked to swim, even on the coldest day, heaving her overweight old body into the waves and turning to peer at me like a big hairy mermaid. Where the retreating sea revealed mussel beds I could spy on turnstone, oyster-catchers, curlew and redshank. I used to discover myself plodding along doing mock-Gregorian chants if nobody was around, and sometimes, embarrassingly, if they were. I used to. But then a man drowned himself in a couple of feet of water behind the sand bar, and I never felt the same about the beach again. The Falklands War had spoilt his life and one Sunday he'd rolled up his anorak neatly on the beach and waded into the pool the tide left, the one children played in because it was safe.

I saw him and thought he was drunk, so passed on, never imagining. When I came back somebody had hauled him out and draped his anorak over his face.

Today I avoided that part of the beach, walking further along to the eastern cliffs because I needed some space between me and death. Larkin called it the 'arrogance of eternity' but it wasn't so much death itself as the method of dying. Oblivion sometimes seemed a positive choice.

By Monday lunchtime I'd decided to hand the photographs to the police. If I had been Mandy I'd have left town and gone somewhere where nobody, including Danny, could find me. It could be weeks, or never, before she turned up and I couldn't stand the thought of having the pictures in the house. I'd removed them from my coat and hidden the packet under Daisy's basket, but every time I passed it the pictures beamed like holograms. I didn't even want them near my dog.

Less than an hour later I was back, the packet still in my pocket. I'd dreaded bumping into Sue's Plod, but I hadn't reckoned on being turned back by another face that I didn't want to see either. What is it about police stations? You step through the street door into Kafkaland, all the little guilts of your insignificant life magnified into criminal proportions – even though you know that the women and men with all that power have *their* little guilts, and some big ones too. As I waited for the duty officer in the reception area the heavy door between me and the inner sanctum opened and shut to let the authorised and the arrested in and out. When I was a reporter it seemed just a means of keeping out the draft; now it had a digital lock on the inside.

As I studied, with the intense concentration of the bored, the public noticeboard warning of the colorado beetle and wanted men, this door was pushed open from the inside by a uniformed Pc in the act of securing his two-way radio to his tunic. He fluffed it and the radio clattered to the floor. He held open the door with his hip as he bent to retrieve it, and over his back I saw a shirt-sleeved Inspector coming down the staircase with a man in street clothes and plasters on his face. The Pc straightened up and let the door click shut behind him. We made it to the street exit at the same time and he courteously let me through first. If there were any 'evening all' coppers left, he looked the part.

Back home I found a new hiding place for the packet: the garden shed was such a mess that I rarely bothered to lock it on the 'no burglar would bother' principal.

Danny rang that evening.

'I found her – what do you want me to do with her?'

He'd made Ricki keep watch on Mandy's new squat and she'd turned up after dark.

I told Jack to forage in the fridge for his supper and went out to the car. The yuppy couple had parked so close I had to drive up on the pavement to get out. I wasn't too careful and scraped their bumper as I got free.

Mandy's story

I expected to find a less-than-happy-Mandy as I blundered out of the black hallway into her den, but whatever she'd mainlined or sniffed or smoked had reduced her to an amiable pliability. It was worse than her hostility.

Ricki was outside keeping an eye on the street and Danny was leaning against the doorless entrance to the room, his face a mixture of boredom and scorn for Mandy. It didn't seem necessary to stand guard on her – she wasn't going anywhere, not tonight anyway.

'What's she said?' I asked him.

'Not a lot. I've been waiting 'til you arrived.'

I crouched down beside her, catching the odour of stale sweat and make-up. She smiled as if I was her bosom pal.

'Lo.'

'Mandy, I need to know what went on at the Sea Chalet.' I felt shitty, she was so vulnerable. 'Who gave you those pictures?'

She turned her head as if it weighed a ton and gazed up at Danny. 'Not with him here.'

Danny lurched off the wall. 'I could do with a breath of fresh air. She stinks. We'll be outside – if she gives you any bother, call us. And you – he thrust his tattooed fist into Mandy's face – 'do as you're fucking well told. You've caused enough trouble.'

'Fuck you,' she whispered to his back. She seemed to have forgotten I was there.

'Mandy –'

'Got a smoke?'

I rolled her one and had to put it into her hand. Her fingers were icy cold. 'Mandy you have to tell me about the Sea Chalet. Did Catterell kill Dulcie?'

She almost missed her mouth with the cigarette and I guided it to her colourless lips. 'I don't have to tell you anything,' she said. 'But I will because he's a bastard. They're all bastards. Do you like men?'

'Some. What did Catterell do?'

I thought she'd fallen asleep: her eyes shut and the

only sounds were from the lamp and the men's low voices outside the basement window.

'Poor old bitch. She didn't know what was going on. They doped her up. I did it for the money but that's different ... I been doing it all my life. It didn't mean the same. But she had to because they made her. That bloody Cockburn, filthy fat pig.'

'The doctor? The gross one in the photos?'

'Yeah, *Doctor* Cockburn, what a joke!'

'And did they kill Dulcie?'

'She was going to tell, wasn't she. All about their little business. You got any dope?'

'How did Dulcie get the photographs?'

Mandy was beginning to shake. 'I need something,' she moaned.

'I'll get you something, but first you have to tell me.'

'John done it. I know it was him because he made a joke about it – about she was round the bend and the bleach cleaned right round the bend like it said on the telly. The wally.'

'But why?'

She looked at me like she had once before, as if I was stupid. 'She'd nicked the bloody pictures hadn't she. And she wouldn't tell them where they were. But Sid knew. She'd given them to him to show the police. She was cute enough to do that.' Mandy's humourless laugh triggered off a coughing fit. My legs were cramped so I sat down beside her and waited until she got her breath back.

'How did they find out about Sid?'

'How'd you think? If someone held a bottle of bleach up to your mouth you'd tell them what they wanted to know – well I bloody would. Course she told.'

'But John killed her anyway, even though she told them she'd given Sid the photographs?'

Mandy was getting tired of me. 'Yeah, yeah. She was a nutter. She'd have told on them all. What about the fix?'

I knew she'd stay put while I asked Danny for some stuff. When I came back she took an interminable time rolling the joint.

'This all he got? The bastard.'

'It'll have to do for now.' I said. 'Let's get on with this: why was Sid murdered?'

'Christ, you never give up do you?' She took a deep drag on the cigarette and closed her eyes, holding in the smoke. 'He wouldn't tell them at first.' She let the smoke escape in a slow luxurious plume. 'He was a nice old bloke actually. Thought the world of Dulcie. They was going to get married, did you know? John was supposed to find out where the pictures were but he got a bit rough and Sid couldn't take it, poor old sod.'

'And anyway he'd given you the photographs?' I prompted.

'Yeah, I'd got the photographs. My passport out of there. My chance to make a bit of money. They been making it out of me. I been used all my life. I'm sick of being other people's meal ticket, so I ran – and then I phoned Catterell and told him, hand over the money or I'm posting the pictures to Scotland Yard.'

I didn't know whether I believed her about Sid handing over the pictures. Why would he?

'I didn't steal them if that's what you think,' she said. 'I had to make his bed because he was paralysed down one side and couldn't do it. They hide things under their mattresses – bottles, pills they're supposed to have taken – and we're supposed to look. When I found the pictures he was in a right state. Dulcie'd told him to hand them over to MI5 and he didn't know what to do.'

'But *you* did,' I said, more pointedly than I'd intended.

Mandy looked at me defensively. 'Not at first. I didn't want him to get into trouble.'

'He couldn't have got into much more trouble,' I pointed out. 'What did they do with his body?'

She shook her head. 'I don't know. I wasn't supposed to know anything about it – wasn't even supposed to know he was dead, but John was scared of what he done because he wasn't supposed to have done it. I got it out of him in the end.'

I was impressed, not just by her compassion for the old man but also for her bravery. 'Weren't *you* scared?' I asked her. 'I'd have been.'

'Bloody right! But so was that slimeball Catterell. He didn't know where to find me so he sent John with the money to the Post Office number I give him. He couldn't trace me – 'til the other night.'

'Danny saved you then,' I reminded her.

'You think the sun shines out of his arsehole don't you,' she said suddenly. 'But he's only in it for what he can get. He's like all the rest.'

I could see that for her I wasn't any better.

'You got what you want,' she added. 'You taken my pictures. I earned those.' The hostility, which had never really left her eyes, flared out at me.

There wasn't much point asking how much Catterell had paid her to pose for him: it wouldn't have been for love. The only money I had on me was the child benefit I'd collected that morning. She took it.

'They're worth a lot more than that,' she sniffed, crumpling the few notes into her pocket.

'I know,' I said. 'But nobody's going to make money out of them any more.' As if that was some consolation to her. 'What will you do now?'

'What's it to you?'

'Some people do care, Mandy. Your probation officer for one. She wants you to get in touch with her.'

Mandy laughed gloomily: 'I bet.'

'She wants you to get help at the Drug Centre.'

Mandy choked on the joint. 'What for! You lot've got no idea have you! You got your nice cosy little homes, your nice boring little jobs. You think you're so frigging superior.' She looked at me slyly. 'Do your posh friends know you're a dyke?'

She looked really calculating and it dawned on me that she might be thinking of blackmailing me as well.

'And what about you in that picture, with Dulcie?' I said it before I could stop myself.

'That's different. I'm not a lezzie – and even if I was nobody'd give a shit. Not like you.'

She had me there, but she'd also got my wild up. 'Different? You're damn right – you do it for money. You do it so that the men you hate can wank off watching you. And the world calls that "natural"! I do it for love and that's 'perversion'. Who do you think's right, Mandy?' I hadn't meant to get angry, not with her. Later I regretted it even more.

Our raised voices brought Danny back into the

basement. 'What's going on – she giving you trouble?'

Outside, as I was leaving, I asked him to go easy on her. He threw up his hands in mock surrender. 'You're the boss.'

'In that case, see if you can get her somewhere else to live – somewhere miles away. One of those men who attacked her on Saturday night was in the police station today having a cosy chat with an Inspector.'

Sic(k) transit

Women's energies are diverted in so many directions, most of them for somebody else's benefit, that it's a miracle we ever leave anything to posterity. Our achievements trickle like spilt milk into corners and cracks that nobody ever sees but everybody knows exist, so long as they don't have to acknowledge them. Could Shakespeare have transcended the barriers of time and culture if he had the prolific stomach contents of a 15-year-old to be cleaned up, a dog with a bulbous blood-filled ear needing attention, food to be bought, cooked and then scraped off greasy plates? Not that I was about to produce a Lear, but lately my own writing had dwindled in quality and quantity , and if I thought about it at all it was with dread.

When I got back from Mandy's I walked in to find Jack with his head down the toilet bowl, and Daisy with her head at a peculiar angle. Jack puking is a thing apart: if dinosaurs had orgasms they probably sounded not unlike him. I got him to bed after the last primeval heave and took his temperature. It wasn't bordering on the fatal but it was high. His face felt like hot wet suet and his teeth were chattering. He swallowed a couple of painkillers with water that stayed down about 15 minutes before putting in a spectacular reappearance, and then proceeded to bark up what seemed like the last six days' consumption of food pretty well every hour on the hour throughout the rest of the night.

Daisy's ear which I had been treating for canker was

twice its normal size, and its distinctive smell wafted about the house, mingling with the Savlon in Jack's sick bowl. I gave her a couple of painkillers as well, forcing them to the back of her throat and holding her muzzle shut until she had to swallow. I thought about taking a couple myself but decided they'd spoil the generous dose of Hungarian red that I'd prescribed earlier.

When I got to bed my mind was revving up on temperatures, vet's bills, and Mandy. I couldn't remember where I'd got to with the list but it was somewhere around Q. Queen this and that seemed like cheating so I started on R. For Josephine Ruffin, although I couldn't remember why, Miriam Rothschild, Adrienne Rich, Lee Remick, Sheila Rowbotham . . .

By 3.20 and yet another stumble into Jack's bedroom to hold his head and empty the bowl, I had included Elaine Showalter, Dale Spender, Mary Seacole, Olive Schreiner, Mother Teresa, Sojourner Truth, Harriet Trubman and Maria van Trapp (if anybody deserves re-evaluation she does). . .

By morning I was wrecked. Jack was sleeping the sleep of the innocent and exhausted, and Daisy was rolling on her back in the hallway, smacking her legs – and ears – onto the walls. I rang the vet and made an appointment for later that morning. My brain was in there somewhere, under a glutinous coating of what felt like slug slime, or I'd have thought about Sue, but I didn't and it was too late when I did. If our paths crossed, so be it. I treated my liver to a pint of cold orange juice and stuffed muesli absent-mindedly into my mouth while listening to Brian Redhead being amiable to yet another Government spokesman who was the only one in step. Nobody ever understood what the Government was trying to do: not the Church, the teachers, social workers, the CBI, Shelter, the NHS, the GPs, the Arts, not even the Army, and certainly not the great British public. I wished I had his blind and ignorant confidence. He was either a charlatan or a fool and, in his case, probably both. I showed the vacuum cleaner the livingroom carpet, which I hadn't finished paying for, bunged a wash into the machine which also hadn't been paid for, and hosed down the backyard. As I shovelled Daisy's bowel contents into a bucket I pondered on the notion that women were delicate, lovely creatures who didn't like getting their hands dirty. 'Sugar and spice' and all that. I stopped pondering when I got the bleach out from under the sink for the dog bucket.

Daisy knew. All the way to the vet's she kept trying to draw me in different directions, and when we got into reception she hid under my chair, her body quivering. I was a bit quivery too, trying to remember if this was Sue's day off or on, and how I would handle it if she was there. And then there she was, in the doorway, calling out for 'Daisy Hills' as if I was the dog's mother. Her voice was coldly professional when she said 'Come this way please', as if I didn't know the way into surgery. She was nice to Daisy, stroking her head and holding her steady while the vet examined her, but I just might as well not have been there. Daisy banged her tail on the floor and shivered, torn between pleasure at a friendly voice and terror of the vet. It was awkward when both of us had to crouch beside the dog while Mrs.Bennet poked around in one of Daisy's ears. Our hands inadvertently touched as we soothed her, but Sue's indifference was arctic and I was so hot with embarrassment that my assumed casualness must have been transparent. If Mrs Bennet was aware of the atmosphere she didn't show it. She stood up, waving aside my apology for the puddle Daisy had left on the floor, and taking what seemed like a month to explain why it was necessary for her to operate and what to do with Daisy between now and 8.45 the next day when I should bring her back.

Sue saw us out, efficient and apparently detached, and the door shut on us, leaving me experiencing a mixture of relief and resentment. On the way home I chided myself for caring one way or the other, but I couldn't deny that I would have liked someone to confide in – and that, in the past, had been Sue.

Jack was awake when I got back, and his temperature was still high, his eyes were feverish and the gland in the left side of his neck was as big as a pullet's egg, so I phoned our doctor. He arrived at lunchtime and diagnosed glandular fever of the less dramatic variety for which, he said, he couldn't do anything. Cool drinks, paracetamol and time would sort Jack out.

'And how about you, Mrs Hills?' he asked as we went down the stairs. He always called me Mrs even though he knew the title didn't apply. I suppose he thought it more complimentary than Miss under the circumstances, and couldn't bring himself to say Ms. 'You're not looking your usual self.'

Since I only ever saw him when death seemed a distinct possibility I assumed I was a picture of health.

'Still smoking?'

'Not a lot,' I lied.

He gave me one of his 'meaningful' looks. 'There's no such thing – you either are or you aren't.'

'Then I am.'

He tutted and snapped his case shut, a touch peevishly I thought, but I was used to his funny little ways. Years ago he used to intimidate me; now I thought of him as a patronising old fart.

When he'd gone I made Jack comfortable and went out to buy Indian tonic and more paracetamol. Moving about among the other shoppers I had an odd sense of unreality, of going through the motions of normality.

That skinny little girl

By 8.45 next morning Daisy and I were back at the vet's. She'd known something was up when she didn't get her breakfast, and all the way there she kept looking up at me with worried eyes. I felt like a traitor and by the time I handed her over to Sue I felt too much distress to feel embarrassed.

'She'll be alright,' said Sue. She meant to be reassuring but it just made things worse. I fled before I made a fool of myself.

The phone was ringing as I put my key in the door and for a moment I imagined it was Sue taking pity on me. But it wasn't.

'Miss? It's Danny.' Something started hammering in my throat. 'I was going to sort her out, honest, but, like, they got to her first. Sorry, right?'

'What're you talking about?' It came out as a croak.

'Mandy, miss. Somebody done her in.'

The world did a quick sidestep and for a few seconds I actually couldn't hear what he was saying.

'Wait a minute,' I interrupted him. 'You're telling me what?'

Mandy had been found the previous night by a man who had gone fishing near the sewage outflow on one of the beaches. He'd discovered a syringe beside her body.

'They tried to make it look like she OD'd but that's not true,' Danny said. 'Ricki was going to drive her to Birmingham where I got friends and she was all for it. Looking forward to getting out of here, you know?'

'Maybe it was a mistake.'

'No way! She knew what she was up to.'

I thought of Mandy slumped in Mira's bathroom, and wondered whether Danny was looking for an easy out, something that didn't point the finger at him.

'She'd come pretty close to it before,' I said.

'She wanted to get out of this place, not out permanent. I told you.'

I couldn't think what to say. I needed time and automatically looked round for Daisy before I remembered where she was. Jack started calling from his room.

'Look Danny, I have to go. Give me a number where I can reach you and I'll call back.'

I wrote the number in a shaky scrawl and put the phone down. All the time I was getting Jack a cold drink and plumping up his pillows, I was thinking of that skinny little girl. She hadn't been much older than my son. There must be somebody worrying about where she was. A parent. Maybe not. Hadn't she said she'd been used all her life? Did that mean –

'Mum!'

The glass in my hand was tipped and tonic was spilling onto the duvet.

Why had they killed her?

'Put the telly on, mum.'

86

The box was near the window and as I pushed the 'on' button next door's white cat launched itself off the wall onto the shed roof. They hadn't needed to kill her to find out what she'd done with the photographs. She had no reason not to tell them.

'Mum, come out the way – I can't see.'

I went downstairs and began checking the locks. The previous owner of the house had been an elderly woman on her own and she'd had small bolts fitted on every door in the house. I used to regard them as an amusing eccentricity.

In the kitchen I took down the earthenware jug that held bread and carving knives, and I knew instantly that I couldn't use any of them, not on living flesh. I poked the jug to the back of the cabinet, and went to the cupboard under the stairs. The light bulb had gone so I had to root around in the dark before I found what I was looking for. In among the squash rackets and cricket gear was on old putter that Jack and I used to knock around with when he was little. I took it upstairs and put it next to my bed. Then I made sure Jack's window was locked and told him not to open it.

'Because,' I told him, 'you'll catch cold on top of every-thing else.'

When I rang the vet's to find out how Daisy was the nurse said she was still whoozy from the anaesthetic and might have to stay in overnight if she didn't come round within the next hour. Selfishly I willed Daisy to wake up: she might be old and fat but she'd got a big deep bark.

In the garden I chopped kindling, carried in the splint-ery sticks and logs – and the hatchet which I hid under the stairs. I wouldn't be able to use it, but neither would anybody else.

It was beginning to rain so I went back into the garden to collect the washing. Next door left was taking hers in but she neither saw nor heard me. She *was* 87. Next door right was in darkness. On a Wednesday she stayed at her sister's because her husband was on night shift and she didn't like being in the house on her own. Opposite our terrace, next to the new houses, was a derelict primary school that the county council had shut down because there were less than 30 kids to a class. Mrs. Next door right hadn't been able to face Wednesday nights alone since a dosser had stumbled out of the empty school one night and leant on her Bells of St Mary's door chimes before collapsing on her doorstep. It had given her, she said, a nasty turn. And who was I to sneer?

An hour later I made Jack promise not to answer the door or the phone while I went to collect Daisy – she'd just about returned to the land of the living when I called the vet's and I wanted to get round there before they changed their minds about letting her go. She had to be lifted into the back of the car and out of it once we got home. Huge stitches were poking out of her right ear flap and she was trembling. I got a blanket and tucked it round her and within minutes she appeared to be sleeping although there was a curious rumbling in her throat. She didn't even hear the lifeboat maroon that usually made her jump up barking. I jumped for both of us and went in search of something soothing. The wine was cold and sour but I drank it anyway as I lit the fire and pulled the curtains against the darkening sky.

Nothing happened that night. It never does when you're expecting it. Daisy and Jack slept right through while I lay awake listening to an ominous plopping noise in the loft, and watching headlights race along the ceiling. Whenever I started to drift off a surge of adrenaline startled me back to consciousness. Once, a car pulled up outside and the engine rumbled on until I sneaked to the window and eased back the curtain. The street lamps were out and I couldn't see what make it was before the car pulled away. I checked on Jack and Daisy, who wagged her tail weakly, and then went back to my bed.

On the trail of the loathsome swine

The alarm broke up a confusing dream. I couldn't remember the details, but its oppressive atmosphere stayed with me for the rest of the day. So did the tea-coloured stain on the bedroom ceiling that meant more roof slates were coming loose. It would have to wait – Daisy's operation had set me back £70. I thought about cancelling the mammograph I'd booked for 10.30 but there wasn't much point. I wouldn't get the money back and it was three years since the last one.

Jack was awake and feeling better so I got him to stand at the bottom of the loft ladder while I handed down the assortment of bowls and buckets that had been catching rain since winter set in. I emptied the dirty water down the loo and repositioned the containers under a roof that was showing daylight in several places.

Daisy was looking sorry for herself but her stomach had recovered enough to handle a roll of brawn and a shovelful of biscuits. When I left she and Jack were curled up together on the sofa watching television.

I was jumpy all the way to the hospital, convinced that every car spending more than three minutes behind me was on my tail. One did follow me most of the way but turned off two streets before the hospital. The car park was full and the waiting room crowded. I checked in and stood in the corridor reading the notices. The hospital needed a million pounds for neo-natal babies in the intensive care unit. The Friends of the Hospital were holding a boot fair to buy comforts for the patients. Great Ormond Street had an appeal going. The corridor needed painting, the casualty unit shut at midnight, and junior doctors were still working dangerously-long shifts.

'Miss Hills?'

Two women were in front of me, one on a couch having her breasts examined by a nurse, the other having hers squashed in the x-ray machine. I winced, remembering how it felt.

Within 15 minutes I'd been x-rayed, the disparity in my breast sizes remarked upon, and ushered out the door. Every time I have to visit hospital I come away feeling more microbe than human. When I was expecting Jack I heard myself described by a male gyneacologist as an 'elderly primate'.

I stomped back to the car and on an impulse headed in the direction of the Sea Chalet. Maybe it was feeling like a microbe, or maybe I was looking for inspiration. Or maybe I was being just plain stupid. I drew up in a side-street from where I could see the hostel. It looked like all the others: no neon sign advertising 'murders our speciality', nothing to distinguish it from the rest, and when the front door opened and James Catterell appeared he didn't leap out in a white coat wielding a camcorder. I slumped down in the driving seat, watching him through the steering wheel and wondering what he'd do if he saw me. He came halfway down the steps and then went back to assist a little group of residents onto the pavement. He was really solicitous the way he lent his arm to a Down's Syndrome woman, depositing her carefully on the pavement before returning to give similar help to an older man. He'd probably done the same for Sidney before he unleashed his human pitbull on him. When the group set off in the direction of the seafront, holding hands like children, Catterell stepped into the road to get into the driving seat of his left-hand drive Mercedes. I had a brief fantasy about stamping on the accelerator and ramming him, of seeing his terrified face as I hurtled down on him, the expensive briefcase bursting open and scattering his stinking secrets over the street.

When he left I followed him, trying to stay a couple of cars behind. His first stop was another hostel and I wondered if he owned that too. He was inside for about 10 minutes. After that he stopped on double yellows outside a bank and I thought resentfully that he'd got away with it until a traffic warden strolled up and started walking round the Mercedes as if it was the biggest affront to the highway code he'd ever encountered. I waited with pleasure the pulling-out of the penalty book, but Catterell spoilt it by coming back. And then it was like they were long-lost brothers and instead of giving him a ticket, the warden slapped him on the shoulder and sloped off to spoil someone else's day.

Catterell made one other stop before I realised that this was a waste of time. What had I hoped to gain from following him, anyway? All I was doing was using petrol. When he pulled in to the side entrance of an estate agents I drove past slowly, trying to watch him and the traffic. He had a car phone clamped to his ear.

The Probation Office wasn't far so I called in and asked to see Mandy's PO. I might not be able to go direct to the police, but maybe I could slide in through the backdoor. In any case, somebody had to be warned about places like the Sea Chalet taking on young offenders.

'She's moved,' said the woman on reception.

I stared at her stupidly. 'Moved?'

'To another area.'

'What about Bill – he's still here?'

'Of course he is,' she laughed, as if the very idea was preposterous. 'But he's not in, not until Monday. He's away at a conference.'

I declined her offer to see somebody else, and left. I needed to know who I was speaking to before I spilled the beans on Catterell. Monday seemed a long way off.

Appropriate actions

On the way home I noticed a newsagent's billboard proclaiming in big black handwriting ANGLER FINDS GIRL'S BODY ON BEACH

I pulled up and bought a copy of the rag. The story was a few paras on the front page:

A late-night fisherman
fought a life-and-death
battle to save a young
woman on the beach near
Simpson's Gap on Tuesday.
Mr Les Denny, a St John
Ambulance Brigade member,
made his heroic attempt
when he spotted the body
near the sewage outfall.
'I tried artificial re-
suscitation,' Mr Denny
told a reporter, 'but the
young lady didn't respond
and I called the police.'

91

Mr Denny said he thought
she may have died of a drug
overdose because he found a
used hypodermic syringe near
the girl's hand.
Police have identified the
dead woman as 19 year old
Mandy Pasmore who was well-
known in the area as a
squatter. They say foul play
is not suspected.

Well they would wouldn't they, I thought bitterly. Still
there was bound to be an inquest and I wondered if I
could chance sending the photographs to the Coroner.

I went home feeling a bit more hopeful.

'Sue rang,' said Jack. 'Oh yeah, and some bloke.'

'Who?' The hammer was back in my throat.

'Dunno, he didn't say.'

'Well *what* did he say?'

Something about tell your mother to send back the pictures when she's finished having a good look at them.
What's for lunch?'

Panic pushed its spiky snout into my voice: 'How did
he know I was your mother?'

'Don't have a go at me!' Jack yelled. 'He thought I was
your husband. What was I supposed to say? What's
wrong with that?'

They knew. They knew about Jack. I saw him cycling
to school one day and his body smashed off the road by
a hit-and-run driver. I saw him kidnapped and his ear
sent through the post in a box.

'Nothing,' I said.

'That's alright then,' my son growled. 'What about
something to eat – I'm starving.'

They'd won. They would get away with murdering
three people and there wasn't a thing I could do about it.
I hadn't felt this alone since returning to an empty house
with a new baby. I'd needed somebody around then –
not Mark, although even he would have been someone
to share the enormous responsibility with. Mark! I shot

into the study and found his emergency-only number in my diary. He wouldn't like it, but that was tough.

He wasn't there, of course, so I left a message on his answerphone asking him to ring me immediately. Then I got worried about everybody else close to me. If they'd been watching me they might know about Sue.

'It's me,' I said when she answered her phone.

'Yes, thank you for ringing back.' She sounded ready to be offended so I decided to say nothing. 'Don't you think it's about time we had a talk?'

Suddenly I felt tired of the game. People were dying. I meant to say something profound and memorable. Instead I said 'Like what – ships and kings and police-women and things?' I regretted it even before I'd finished. There was a time when I told Sue everything – well, almost everything. I needed her now more than she needed me. Just to prove it I put the phone down.

It rang almost immediately. 'Miss Hills?'

I knew that voice. 'Who is it?'

'You're being very silly Miss Hills. There's a name for women who follow people going about their normal business. They call it sick obsession.'

'You ignorant bastard!' I snarled.

'Now, now, Miss Hills. Be a sensible girl. You've stolen something and I think you ought to return it.'

It was an odd way of saying it, and I wondered whether he thought I might be taping the conversation. He'd that devious sort of mind. I wished I'd thought of it first.

'Look Catterell' - I deliberately used his name just to make him less smarmy – 'I don't know what you're talking about. What is it you want back?'

His voice dropped: 'You're playing stupid games. Somebody could get hurt.'

He was right. I thought of Jack out in the traffic. 'Okay, but you have to give me a couple of days. I put them somewhere safe. It'll take a while to get them.'

Catterell thought about it. 'Alright, but don't take too long. I'm a patient man, Miss Hills, used to dealing with difficult people' (he meant 'loonies') 'but if the property isn't returned to its rightful owner by, let's say, Monday, I shall take the appropriate action.'

It all sounded legal, the way he put it, but I didn't doubt he meant something a lot more terminal than a letter from his solicitor.

I was shaking badly and hoped Jack wouldn't notice as I passed him on the way to the kitchen. He didn't even look up.

Trembly hands are perfect for scrambling eggs – not so good pouring orange juice. All the time I was stirring the egg and mopping up the juice my mind was on the packet in the shed. Once Catterell had it there wasn't any evidence left. I could hardly pop into Boots and order copies. Dulcie's notes didn't amount to any more than the egg I was burning. Her references to J.C. would be interpreted as Jesus Christ not James bloody Catterell. Ring, Mark, damn you!

He got through at just after nine o'clock, and Jack got to the phone first.

'It's Mark,' was all he said, although he knew who and what Mark was.

The line from Brussels was clearer than most local ones. 'I've just got in – what's the matter?'

'Nothing really,' I said. 'I want you to have Jack for a couple of weeks. I need a break.'

Half an hour later he gave in. I didn't tell him the real reason because his bureaucrat brain wouldn't have been able to accept it. Things like that didn't happen in Mark's world where everything had its place and there was a place . . . etc. And even if he had been able to imagine an England where people got murdered by pornographers, I didn't want a sermon on my inefficiency in getting involved with them – or a reminder of my selfishness in having a child that Mark hadn't wanted in the first place. Instead, I told him Jack was unwell and needed a break as much as I did. I got the sermon on my unwarranted motherhood, anyway, and I let him drone on a bit before we got down to details. The longest he could take Jack was nine days, then he had to go to Switzerland, or Swaziland or somewhere. He would drive to Ostende and pick Jack up from the ferry on Saturday night. It was all very inconvenient and the Common Market would collapse without him but he at least had a sense of responsibility etc etc . . .

Jack was not exactly thrilled at having to go to 'boring old Brussels' and stay with 'boring old Mark' whom he'd only met three times in his entire life, not when he could stay here and be with his mates. Then I reminded him that Mark was rather well-off and would probably take him shopping for clothes because he'd be too ashamed to be seen with him in the flash restaurants they'd probably be eating in. Jack began to get more enthusiastic about the idea and went upstairs to sort out his laundry while I answered the phone. It was Maureen.

Her parents had offered to have the children at their place on Saturday night and would I like to go out – 'Scandles, or somewhere?'

I wasn't sure what the invite meant: did it include the other women, or just Maureen and me? I wasn't sure what I wanted it to mean but when she said 'The others will probably be there' I had my usual cocktail of reactions – regret laced with relief, and then a slice of anxiety that Sue might be there with her Plod in tow, chased down with a dash of rebellion against my own wimpishness. I didn't actually want to go to Scandles but the only other gay club was out in the country, was expensive and meant I'd have to drive.

Celebration

Even before I kissed Jack goodbye and waved him onto the boat, I had grave misgivings about what I was doing. What if I couldn't get this sorted out before he got back? What if he was followed on the boat? What if –

'Mum, you're embarrassing me!'

I let him out of the bear hug, warned him about talking to strangers – 'Particularly men. Don't smirk' – and he joined the queue shuffling through the boarding hall.

'And don't drink going over,' I shouted after him. He turned and raised an imaginary glass and then was lost in the crowd. I swallowed a lump and fought my way to the phone booths. By the time the taxi arrived the ferry was pulling out in a blaze of light that reflected on the oily black sea around the terminal. It was one of those times for religion and I hadn't got any. I thought of cancelling my night out and then thought how it would be spending the evening on my own, sitting around waiting for Mark's all-clear from Ostende. Gill looked at me quizzically as Maureen and I joined the group in the upstairs bar. I knew what the look meant, but I wasn't in the mood to explain. She had other ideas.

'You look terrible,' she said, drawing me aside. 'Haven't you sorted it out yet?'

For a mad moment I thought she was referring to the Sea Chalet.

Gill sighed. 'I don't know what's the matter with you both. Sue downstairs with someone else, you're up here with – are you *with* Maureen? What's going on?'

She wasn't just being nosy. I gave her a hug. 'People get tired of one another, Gill. Stop worrying.' That, from me, was a joke.

She shook her head in disbelief. 'I thought you –'

'I know,' I said. 'But we can't go on being the token couple just to please everybody.'

I knew how Gill felt. Long-term relationships were spanners in the works of homophobia. I followed her gaze to where Rachel was talking to another woman. 'You don't need us,' I told her.

'You don't understand,' she said. 'I love you and Sue. You really piss me off sometimes.'

For all my rationalising in the bar, I avoided looking Sue's way when we went downstairs. And when the slow numbers came up I kept a slight distance between my body and Maureen's. She didn't force the issue, not even when I kept glancing at my watch. I was willing the time to go faster, seeing in my mind the ferry drawing agonisingly slowly through the night; and Mark who, at that moment, represented Jack's safety, waiting on the quay.

Maureen put her mouth close to my ear: 'You're miles away.'

'I'm not very good company tonight.'

She stepped back a pace and looked at me, smiling. 'No, you're not – but it's okay.'

At 11.30 I was on the phone. By 11.35 I was back downstairs feeling stones lighter. Jack was stuck into steak and chips in a restaurant opposite their hotel – and was it true I let him drink beer? Because Mark didn't think much of it if I did.

'Give him two,' I said. 'And don't be such a kill-joy.'

I'd put the phone down before Mark could deliver his second sermon of the week, and almost skipped to the bar to order a bottle of plonk. I felt so good I didn't even mind standing next to Plod who was waiting to be served. Politely she made room for me but avoided eye contact, which was difficult because there was a mirror at the back of the bar in which we could both see ourselves. She had to be at least 10 years younger than Sue, although I suspected that the attraction was her air of confidence rather than her youth. Or was I just telling myself that? There wasn't anything objectionable about her, except maybe her tendency to laugh a lot, and even that must have made a change from me. I stood aside while she manoeuvred a tray of drinks off the counter and she said 'Thanks'. It was all very civil and I made a promise not to keep thinking of her as Plod.

God knows why I felt so magnanimous. My small coup in putting Catterell off for a couple of days and getting Jack out of harm's way was just breathing space. Hardly a victory over the forces of evil.

'What're we celebrating?' Jackie stood up to make space for me next to Maureen.

'What would you like to celebrate?'

'Tax-free tampons.'

'Andrea Dworkin in the White House,' Ellie shouted.

'All homosexual Tory MPs who let Clause 28 through to be outed,' said Gill.

'What about you?' I asked Maureen.

'I'd settle for a pleasant evening.' She looked at me steadily and put her arm round my shoulders. 'How about you?'

I couldn't tell her what I wanted to celebrate. It was too complicated and I didn't want to think about it right then anyway. I poured wine into her glass. 'I'd like to celebrate forgetfulness, even if it's only for a little while.'

On the dance floor I closed the gap between us. Her body moved under my hand in the small of her back and her head was warm against mine. I shut my eyes and my mind and let myself slide into the music.

Sex in the head

An hour later we were walking on the beach in the first snow flurry of the winter; six of us arm in arm doing a Tiller routine in the freezing sand, the wind flinging salt and snow into our mouths as we sang our version of 'Stand by your man'. We danced along the edge of the sea, getting caught in the tide, screaming as the waves sped over the tops of our shoes. There was something pagan about being out in the night, the lights of the town like blossom in the blurred distance, the ocean a constant roar, the fine stinging atoms of sand in the tickertape snow.

I didn't want it to end. I wanted to go on for ever in this dark crazy night, but I fell back when I realised we were nearing Simpson's Gap. Maureen dropped back too.

'Had enough?' she asked.

I stepped towards her and pulled her to me. Her mouth was warm and alive.

'Let's go back,' I said.

We called to the others, but the wind tore our voices away, and they disappeared into the darkness.

It seemed like five but was probably nearer 30 minutes when we got back to Maureen's flat. It had been a long time since I'd felt such hunger for someone and my movements were fluid and accurate as I undressed her. Hers were no less. We moved into one another and the world became a hot, smooth dream of pleasure.

And then into my mind like a stabbing light was the picture of Dulcie, surrounded by men in white coats, manipulating her for the camera and for the eyes of men for whom her powerlessness meant pleasure. I tried to shut out the tableau and lose myself in the here and now, but the pictures kept appearing, like flashes on a screen. I sat up, angry and afraid, violated by the images.

'Mig?' Maureen hadn't moved. I put out my hand in the dark and felt her fingers grip mine. 'Is it Sue?'

I shook my head, not trusting my ability to speak, then leant over and switched on the light as if that would drive out the pictures. I wanted to tell her why it had happened – I owed her that – but I felt contaminated, my sexuality invaded by sick distortions. I wasn't even thinking of Maureen really: what I was thinking was whether I'd be able to make love again without seeing another woman's degradation. I shivered and Maureen sat up, pulling the blanket around my shoulders. She lit a cigarette and put it between my lips. 'I'll make some tea,' she said.

One foot in front of the other

As soon as it was light I walked home. It took me nearly an hour and when I got in I couldn't stay put. The house felt cold and empty. I picked up Daisy's lead and she galloped to the front door, ecstatic even though she hadn't had her breakfast. I drove out to the reserve and walked along the seapath, glad that nobody else was up and about. The windows of the hide were open but nobody was inside. Vandals had smashed the lock, slashed the bird charts on the walls and deliberately left the hut open to the weather. I shut the windows, wedged the door to with a chunk of stone, and caught up with Daisy. Instead of turning back at the edge of the marsh we headed down the track to the river. The tide was out and most of the birds had left the shelter of the reeds and glasswort for their feeding grounds. When I got to the edge of the river and the deep mud I stopped. Near the marsh the mud was only an inch or so deep, but as the land sloped towards the river the ooze deepened and walking was amost impossible. Daisy had once got herself trapped and it took Sue and me all our combined strength to get her, and ourselves, out.

Daisy was wagging her tail and looking at me questioningly. I stared across the river at the spit of sand on the far side where great black backs and cormorants rested at high water, and on out into the Channel towards Belgium. Jack and Daisy seemed at that moment to be the only reality worth holding onto.

Daisy was making encouraging noises in her throat. I looked down at my best black leather boots.

'Come on then,' I said, and stepped out into the mud.

I can understand, I think, why people tramp the countryside, unable to stay in one place. Walking was a kind of therapy, the only normal thing to do that morning; to keep putting one foot in front of the other and going until you couldn't go any further. We slopped our way through the shallow stuff until we reached the firmer flats of the bay, scattering mallard and shelduck that took off as if looking for a livingroom wall to cling to. Baitdiggers were carving horseshoe shapes in the rich black seabed, but we steered clear of them and kept on towards the open sea. Daisy chased herring gulls and curlews, her tail rotating like a propellor, and I envied her innocent pleasure. She never caught anything. When we reached the soupy shallow wash she paddled out for a swim and I stood watching her as she swirled and turned, her eyes inviting me to join her. I thought of the Navy man who'd drowned himself in water not much deeper than this.

Swollen clouds were banking up like contusions on the sky, darkening the sea as the wind spread them down the Channel. My feet were wet and cold and I couldn't stop my teeth chattering. I called to Daisy and she lolloped out of the water, shaking herself over my legs. The tide was turning and it followed us towards the shore, speeding as it slopped over the rim that curved across the mud flats

Invasion

I was so frozen into myself when we got indoors that I didn't notice anything different about the house. In the hall I fumbled with numb fingers at the straps on my muddy boots and then gave up, tramping mud through to the kitchen where I switched on the oven before filling the kettle. I pulled down the oven door and stood over it, breathing in the warm updraft. Daisy stood in the doorway, wagging her mudcaked tail. Between making tea and toast I washed her food bowls in the blissfully hot tap water.

'You need a bath,' I told her. She stopped banging her tail on the woodwork. 'Okay – grub first.'

We breakfasted in the steamed-up kitchen, Daisy with her muzzle in a pile of meat and biscuit and me with mine in a tea mug. I switched on the radio and for a few minutes succumbed to the Archers. Pru had suffered a stroke and everybody was worried she might never speak again! I took off my coat and boots and called Daisy up to the bathroom.

The contrast after the heat of the kitchen was almost shocking. I pulled the cord on the wall heater and bent to help Daisy into the bath. While the shower was heating up I leant over to the roller blind to let in some light. One of the casement windows was slightly ajar.

I knew I hadn't left it open.

A lot of confused thoughts ran through my head as I sank back on my knees beside the bath. Automatically I started to soak Daisy's coat, mindlessly checking with one hand that the water wasn't too hot. Then panic leaked like acid and I rammed home the silly little bolt on the bathroom door. Frightened, Daisy jumped out of the bath and stood at my feet making worry noises. I began comforting her, and myself, by telling her it was alright and patting her head before wrenching open the door. The house was silent except for the unintelligible doings of Ambridge in the kitchen. A motorbike snarled by on the street. I leant against the door to give my legs support and waited for my vital organs to resume their normal rhythm.

They'd been here. Looking for the photographs. Going through my things, searching, touching –

I stepped onto the stairwell, unable to make the crossing to my bedroom where the putter was, or go down to the lifeline of the telephone. If somebody was still in the house . . .

I jumped as Daisy nudged past me and grabbed her collar, imagining with the manic rapidity of a speeded-up film how an intruder would disable her – bleach in her eyes, a hatchet blow to her neck, a knife jammed down into her spine. I crashed down the stairs dragging her with me, and ran to the cupboard under the stairs. The hatchet was still there and I grabbed it. The bleach was still under the sink, Ambridge was still wrestling with the problems of sex, Pru and organic yoghurt, and Mr Next door was hammering and banging in his shed like he did every Sunday morning. I dropped Daisy's collar and leant against the worktop. This was crazy. They'd hardly burgle a house in broad daylight when most people were at home. I toured the house, hatchet in hand, increasingly reassured by the natural untidiness in which I lived. Anybody searching for a small package would have a job. I'd been amassing photographs, books, magazines, newspaper cuttings and other clutter for more than 20 years and hardly any of it was neatly kept.

Finally I went to the shed, which was never locked since Jack lost the key. That, too, was in its usual state. I scrambled over the bike bits and garden tools and stuck my hand down the back of some old shelves. My fingers closed on the package and I pulled it out.

'Morning,' called Mr Next door, emerging triumphant from his shed with his latest DIY creation. 'What d'you think?'

He held aloft something in wood that could have been a kitchen cabinet. I peered at it through the rose trellis.

'Very nice.'

'Just finished it,' he said, as if it was the work of a lifetime. 'For her kitchen.'

'Not yours then?'

He stared at me, uncomprehending, and changed tack. 'Went to the wedding yesterday – just got back an hour ago – not bad going eh? I don't hang about.'

He launched into some dreary details about the A this and the B that. I nodded and smiled and kept inching towards my backdoor. Then it hit me: 'You weren't here earlier, then – this morning?'

'Just said didn't I,' and off he went again, about roadworks and diversions, his wife's uselessness as a navigator, his own planet-shattering skill as a driver. He was just getting warmed up on the superiority of the front-wheel drive, fuel-injected whatsit when I interrupted him: 'That's my phone ringing,' I lied, and slid into the kitchen.

So they could have done it. They hadn't come at night because of the dog, the alarm they'd wrongly supposed would alert the neighbours. They must have waited until Daisy and I had left this morning. That meant they'd followed me from Maureen's flat.

I raced through to the phone and searched frantically for Danny's number. Catterell didn't trust me to return the photographs. Maybe he'd seen me putting Jack on the ferry and suspected my intentions. If the package wasn't at my place, maybe I'd taken it to Maureen's –

'Yeah?'

'Danny?'

'Who wants him?'

I gritted my teeth. 'It's Mig Hills, his tutor. Just get him, will you.'

'He ain't here.'

The clock on my desk told me I'd been home nearly an hour. Catterell could be at Maureen's now. 'Look you moron, just get him. It's important.'

'Keep your knickers on.'

I listened to the hissing echoes of a hand placed over the receiver which seemed to go on for ever before the monosyllabic drone return: 'He's coming.'

'Wassup?' Danny sounded half-asleep.

'I want you to do me a favour.' I gave him Maureen's address and asked him to make sure someone kept a watch on the flat until I told him differently.

'No prob. What we watching for?'

'The same people who killed Mandy – but you stay out of it, okay?'

He agreed reluctantly. 'I'd like to meet the bloke that done her. That was right out of order.'

I stopped myself commenting that she had been one of his best customers. It wouldn't have been fair and there wasn't time.

Then I rang Maureen. I was relieved, she was confused

and then angry. It was difficult trying to convince her that she might be in danger, and that it was my fault. 'Could you go and stay with your parents?' I asked. 'Or Gill or Ellie?'

Maureen protested, demanding to know what was going on. 'I can't tell you. Just do it, will you, please?'

We went on like this for some minutes before she gave in, saying 'I'm wondering what I've got myself involved in. Is this anything to do with Sue?'

It would have been a convenient lie. I could use the jealous lover bit. I could use Sue.

'In a way,' I said.

Maureen was silent for a while and I cringed at my deceit on behalf of them both.

'I'll go to my parents,' she said at last, and put the phone down.

I wondered who *I* could run to without endangering anyone else. Catterell would be furious that he hadn't been able to find the pictures – or that whoever he'd sent to look for them had returned empty-handed. Who would he have sent? I shuddered at the thought of John peering over my back wall, creeping up a drainpipe and forcing open the bathroom window, sticking his repulsive scalp under the roller blind like some poisonous tortoise.

Enough of that, I thought, and relegated him to the Twilight Zone. I went back upstairs to check for damage to the bathroom window. A lump had been chiselled out of the frame, presumably so that something thin like a knife could be slid under the latch to force it down. Simple and quiet. I pulled the window shut, got a hammer and nails from the shed and secured the latch. They'd have to break the window next time. I sat on the loo seat and thought about the next time. Flooring one of Danny's acned idiots had been one thing – he hadn't been expecting it, and I had. Tackling a psychopath like John was something else, and I didn't want to learn what it was. I needed somewhere safe to stay until tomorrow when I could hand over the pictures to Bill Fletcher. The scenario got a bit fuzzy after that, but it had a happy ending with the villains being arrested and me going off into the sunset, my trusty dog by my side because there was no way I was going to leave her here to the tender mercies of Catterell and Co.

Hide

By mid-afternoon I'd figured it out. The gates into the reserve would be shutting about now, but I knew another way of getting in. It would mean leaving the car about half a mile from where I wanted to be, and hiking along the seawall in the dark. I made a flask of hot soup and filled my backpack with bits to eat, a torch, my binoculars, some candle stubs and, underneath all that, the package.

When I left the house I looked up and down the street to see if anyone was hanging about. The blue of cathode tubes glowed behind curtained windows and there was a smell of chimney smoke in the night chill. If I hadn't been so anxiety-ridden I'd have felt acutely embarrassed, sneaking about like a Michelin man in half a ton of clothing with a rucksack full of goodies as if this was some Blytonesque adventure. Under my wax jacket I wore two thick jumpers and I had on two pairs of socks inside my walking boots.

I parked the car behind a derelict garage on the edge of the bay and spent a few minutes watching the road. Traffic was light and nothing slowed down or showed any sign of interest. One car pulled into the grounds of the pub opposite but when I got the binoculars on the occupants they turned out to be the landlady and her daughter. When I was sure I hadn't been followed I started out for the reserve, keeping Daisy on her lead and continually looking over my shoulder as we drew away from the lights of the pub and the street lamps into the darkness.

The reserve was a different world at night. Wind clicked in the dried-out forests of giant hogweed and the sea smacked its lips against the tumbled rocks that formed the seawall. Small things, startled by the sound of

Daisy's hoarse breathing and my stumbling feet, shot across the narrow path ahead into the safety of wet brambles or the big stones. When a couple of shelduck roosting at the foot of the wall cracked the night with their frantic quacking and shot up beside us I almost fell into the undergrowth with fright, yanking Daisy's neck collar so hard that she yelped. By the time we reached the hide I was hot and out of breath, and convinced that this was one of my more stupid ideas.

I shone the torch into the black interior to make sure nobody was dossing down for the night and stepped inside. While Daisy carried out an inspection with her nose I opened up one of the flaps which gave me a view of the path and sat scanning the area with the binoculars; anybody approaching along the seawall would be silhouetted against the distant lights of the harbour. The weak spot was behind the hide. In ripping off the lock the vandals had made a hole about the size of a fist. I dug into the backpack and pulled out a length of nylon washing line which I threaded through the hole. It was long enough to be tied round one of the bench legs and would hold the door shut – provided somebody didn't cut through it. At least I wouldn't be taken by surprise. I lit the torch and left it on a bench while I went outside; no light showed if all the flaps and the door were shut. Satisfied, I went back in and lashed us in for the night, then spread the contents of the backpack on the floor around me like a table setting so that I could reach whatever I needed fast. Jack's tyre lever lay beside my right hand and a can of his underarm deodorant spray by my left. I lit one of the candles and switched off the torch.

I didn't expect to sleep, and I was right. I couldn't concentrate on the *Guardian* crossword and I'd finished the soup, smoked most of my tobacco and nearly finished the remains of the Christmas Benedictine by 9.45 so I lay down hoping to doze off. I tried the list but couldn't think of any women's names beginning with U. I managed Suzanne Valadon, Agnes Varda and Sarah Winnemucca before I gave up. I was cold and stiff and getting careless, shifting about noisily trying to get comfortable on the hard, drafty floorboards. By 11 o'clock my house was the safest, most comfortable place on earth and I was an idiot. I could have made it secure, I could have been in a nice warm soft bed, and how could I ever have objected to Sue's snoring? She'd be in her bed, but perhaps not alone –

Something crunched on the gravel path outside the door. Daisy jumped up, her iron-hard claws scraping on the boards. I grabbed her collar and clamped a hand over her muzzle. In the light from the candle I could see the washing line vibrating. I jammed my hand onto the flame and sat, paralysed, holding my breath, staring into the darkness.

'Miss Hills.'

The voice was a sing-song whisper.

'We know you're in there.'

Daisy wrenched her jaw free and growled. I could feel her bared teeth as I groped for her head.

'Got your doggy with you, have you? It's a funny time to take it for walkies isn't it? Now why would you do that? Why would you be out here, miles from nowhere, in the middle of the night? Got something to hide Miss Hills?'

I closed my hand over the tyre lever and raised it slowly with an arm that had about as much strength as a wet sock, then let Daisy go and heard her fling herself at the door. With my free hand I groped for the torch: if they broke in I might get time to use the lever while they were blinded by the light.

Over Daisy's barking Catterell had to raise his voice: 'We know the photographs aren't at your house – we've just been over it again, more thoroughly. Why don't you be a sensible woman and hand them over, then we can all get some sleep.'

Shifting the torch into my pocket, I searched for the can of spray, found it, knocked it over, grabbed it and hoped the hole was facing in the right direction.

Catterell gave a deep theatrical sigh: 'Miss Hills, call the dog off – there's really no need. It's simple – you give me my property, I go away, and you can stay out here all winter if you want.'

He was using the sort of voice I imagined he'd use to

cajole a troublesome resident. Like Dulcie maybe. I stood up and moved to the door.

'Is that how you spoke to Dulcie before you had her murdered, you bastard?'

Catterell didn't answer. I could hear him moving about and whispering to someone else. John? Then he came back to the door.

'That's a very serious allegation. I'd say the wild delusion of a neurotic woman – and a hurtful one to me. I take care of my people, Miss Hills, anybody will tell you that.'

'I've seen how you take care of people, Catterell. You get that moron of yours to pump bleach down their throat, or rough them up so that they die, or destroy them with an overdose like Mandy. And then of course,' I added, warming to the subject, 'there's the pornography you make them perform in. It must have really cracked you up when poor old Dulcie snatched those photographs – and even more hurtful when Mandy squeezed your wallet for them. You didn't need to kill her, you pervert – who could she have told about the pictures? Hardly the police.'

Catterell laughed. It was a nasty, sneering, nostrilly sound. 'You don't really believe all that, do you? Dulcie knew what she was up to – she named her price. What *adults* do in private is none of your business – unless, of course, you're one of those women with a problem about sex. Is that it, Miss Hills, eh? Got a hang-up in that department?'

Somebody was moving around the front of the hide. Hogweed was snapping as he felt his way along the top of the slope that dropped away to the seawall.

'I'm not responsible for Dulcie's suicide,' Catterell was saying. 'Old Mr Prince finally plucked up the courage to tell her he didn't want to get married and she couldn't take it. As for Mandy . . . she just got greedy. She'd been paid for her part in our little, shall we say, private parties, and she thought she could blackmail me when she stole the photographs. When I refused to pay she threatened to kill herself – and I did give her some money, to prevent another tragedy. That was my mistake – she presumably blew it on whatever muck she was addicted to and accidentally overdosed.'

Despite the situation I was fascinated by his explanation; it was so feasible. It was the story he'd tell if he had to: a red-blooded man being a bit naughty in the privacy of his own home, unwittingly drawn into the self-destructive worlds of a mad old woman with a hang-up about the Pope and MI5, and a prostitute junkie who was also a thief and an extortionist; then victimised by a neurotic menopausal unmarried lesbian mother. A good barrister could make a lot of that. All Catterell would need would be a dinosaur judge and he'd get probation while I got put away in a nice soft room. His reputation would be slightly tarnished, but what was that to him? He'd bounced back before. He could do it again, if not in this town, then in some other. Even Daisy had stopped barking and seemed to be listening sympathetically.

'Where did Sidney fit in all this?' I asked. 'I'm dying to hear your excuse for his death.'

Catterell tutted: 'Miss Hills,' he said as if talking to a child, 'there's no need to go to such extremes – but then you do, don't you! For your peace of mind I'll explain, although I don't have to.' He broke off and I strained to hear what he was saying to the other person out there. I got my eye to the hole in the door, but all I could see was Catterell's back from the shoulders down. Then he returned to the door and I straightened up. 'As I was saying, Mr Prince's heart was not in good shape. When he heard of Dulcie's death the old chap took a turn for the worse and –'

'Then why did you pretend it was Sidney when I called to see him?'

'Oh dear, oh dear! You are confused aren't you.' Catterell leant against the door as if getting comfortable for a long session. I heard the click of a lighter and smelt cigar smoke. If he had sent John off somewhere and was on his own it would be a good time to make a move. I tip-toed across the the hut and began untying the washing line, keeping it taut so that he wouldn't notice. The door would open outwards and if I hit it hard enough hopefully the smug bastard would be pushed backwards, giving me the chance to make a run for it. I knew the reserve better than him. To the north was a little wooded area where a gate opened onto the main road. If I could make that, there was a farm . . .

'What makes you think it wasn't Mr Prince you saw?' Catterell continued.

Still holding the line tight I groped around for the backpack, slung it over my shoulder, and then moved cautiously back to the door, feeling until I found Daisy's lead. Now I had her lead and the tyre lever in the same hand. If I could smash his head in on the way out, so much the better.

'Because,' I said, 'he died before November 3rd, the date you put in the paper. Mandy knew what had happened. Your gorilla tried to make him hand over the photographs, but he'd already given them to Mandy.'

'All wrong, all wrong,' said Catterell. 'The pictures belonged to Dulcie anyway – she'd asked for a set. Whatever else she was she enjoyed a *normal* sex life, and she liked seeing herself in the photographs. So did the old boy. We think the old are sexless but that's just ageism. She gave those photographs to Sidney and Mandy stole them from him.'

The door creaked as he took his weight off it. 'Now, I think that's enough explaining. Why don't you?

Be a sensible girl?' I suggested. 'If the pictures represent just a bit of harmless fun how come you want them so badly? Why burgle my house and follow me out here?' Gently I took a few steps back and let down the line.

He started to say something, but I didn't hear what it was. Shoulder first I hit the door as hard as I could. I'd expected some resistance as the door smacked into him, but he must have been standing far enough away for it to miss him and bang harmlessly against the hide. My momentum would have carried me several feet up the path but for Daisy's unyielding weight on the end of the lead. Taken by surprise she'd dug her feet in as I shot out the door and I was yanked back into the doorpost. The tyre lever fell from my hand onto the gravel and I was scrabbling for it when Catterell grabbed me. Those fights you see in the cinema are all choreographed; this was more of an unseemly struggle, a confusion of arms and legs and curses as he tried to pin my hands behind my back while I lashed out with my feet and Daisy romped over both of us, snapping at anything that moved. Catterell's weight pushed me onto my knees, throwing him off-balance, and I got my left arm free. For what seemed like a lifetime I was struggling to get the spray can from the pocket I'd stuffed it in. I gave the undergrowth a quick spray before I got it facing the right way, and twisted round trying to find Catterell's face. I found myself looking into John's ugly mug just before I deodorised it. He made the required 'Aaargh!' noises and clapped a hand over his right eye, glaring at me through the one I'd missed, and calling me some unladylike things. Over my laboured breathing I heard Daisy's high-pitched scream. I started to get up, saw Catterell standing over me with the tyre lever raised and tried to duck as it swung down.

My shoulder, neck and head went numb and I knew he'd hit me. I also knew pain was on its way. Then I was on my knees again, leaning on one hand and puking all over his Guccis.

'You mad bitch!' he yelled, and shoved me with one decorated foot onto the gravel where I stayed.

Burn the bitch

All that stuff you hear about passing out with pain – maybe it does happen, but it didn't happen to me. I wished I could faint, just to stop the unrelenting agony, but my brain insisted on seeing the whole performance and the exit doors stayed shut. I was so absorbed in the drama of body damage I didn't care what Catterell and John were up to. I'd even forgotten Daisy. When John hauled me to my feet I recycled more soup and Benedictine over his chest which gained me a punch in the face and a few more vulgar references to my womanhood. He shoved me back into the hide and I went down on the floor like a sack of potatoes.

111

The pain began to subside from a high-key shriek to a baritone throb and I began to see again. Catterell was emptying the backpack and handing the candles to John, who still had a hand over one eye. I couldn't understand why the reptile was placing the stubs around me like I was an enshrined saint, instead of chucking them all over the place. When he started lighting them I tried to sit up to ask what was going on, but my lips seemed to have parted company with my mouth. As the little flames danced around me I noticed Daisy lying just inside the door, her tongue hanging out between her teeth.

'Well Miss Hills – this is what it's all about.'

I couldn't raise my head, but I tipped my eyes sideways to look at Catterell. He was holding the photographs like a hand of cards. He squatted down just outside the circle of lights and leered at me.

'Was it worth it? You've put such a lot of effort into holding on to these that I think you should be allowed to keep them – but not until I've made one or two adjustments.'

He took John's lighter and, holding each picture up in front of me, began setting fire to them and flinging them into my face. 'Like that one do you? Have it! How about this one? – nice pair of tits, Mandy! Pity. Ugly old cunt, wasn't she, our Dulcie? Go on, have a good look.' I shut my eyes as the flaming pictures fluttered down around me.

'Don't go to sleep, you'll miss the fireworks!' Catterell cried, punching the damaged shoulder. I opened my eyes. 'I wouldn't want you to miss the little house-warming we're giving you, seeing as how you like this place so much. Of course, you should be more careful – candles are very dangerous things, especially if you fall on them – like this.'

He pulled me upright by my coat front and onto one of the candles. Before it went out I could smell singeing hair and hot wax.

'See what I mean?' said Catterell. 'And petrol – that's a very dangerous thing too, specially round unprotected lights.'

In answer to my unasked question, John slammed a

can onto the floor about a foot from my face so that I flinched.

'Got the idea, have you?' asked Catterell. 'John's a bit of an old clumsy, as I expect you've noticed. Give him a bottle of bleach or a can of petrol and he's all fingers and thumbs. Aren't you, John?'

Still clutching his face, John picked up the can and then dropped it so that it fell on its side, slopping the reeking contents onto the floorboards.

'It can't be easy with only one eye, poor John,' Catterell crooned, looking at me as if he felt really sorry for me. 'Poor Miss Hills, too. You're going to need a drink. You see,' he said, unscrewing the stopper on the remains of the Benedictine, 'I'm not such an ogre. Now open wide . . .'

There were about two generous measures left in the bottle and he managed to make me choke on most of it.

'Good health!' he said, throwing the bottle behind me and standing up. 'That's about it. It's a sad way to end your life, friendless and alone, but then you're getting to that funny age when women do strange things. Like committing suicide.'

From my floor-level view I could only see the lower half of his legs as he turned away and headed for the door. Behind the legs I could see Daisy lick her lips and I willed her to stay still until they'd left.

The petrol had spread across the boards towards the rear of the hide and the door.

'So long Miss Hills.'

I heard the lighter click and the door bang just before my burning rolled-up *Guardian* dropped onto the petrol. There was a small whoosh and a fence of blue flame danced up between me and the door. Streams of fire rippled over the creosoted boards towards me.

Fear anodysed the pain and I was on my feet. Something fluttered down the front of me and I grabbed it before lurching through the fire to Daisy who was making groggy attempts to get up. I gripped her collar with my with good hand and dragged her kicking to the far side of the hut.

I was gambling on two things: one, that Catterell and John wouldn't hang around because the fire would be

113

spotted from the harbour or the road and they had a good run to get clear of the place; and two, that the fire would eat a hole big enough for me and Daisy to get through before the whole hut went up. None of it was very logical but it was all we'd got. Every breath I took was drawing in searing heat and smoke.

The gap opened up with a great crackling snap as the well-seasoned timber split and the door, which was a sheet of fire, flew open. Daisy was panicking, her one instinct to find a way out, and when she saw it she went for it, with me right behind her.

Her coat was smouldering and I couldn't keep up with her as she tore off into the night. As the hide burst like a bomb I struggled to get out of my wax jacket but couldn't get it off the injured shoulder. I was crying and calling to Daisy at the same time.

By the time the fire brigade and the police got there, the hide was not much more than a glowing skeleton showering the night with sparks. They were very efficient and businesslike, the police. They radioed for an ambulance and it came wailing through the narrow main paths, smashing down the hogweed and adding its flashing lights to those of the fire engine and the patrol car. The air throbbed with the din of engines and radio calls, and figures passed in and out of my vision like something out of hell.

'She keeps asking about a dog,' somebody said.

'Anybody seen a dog?' .

'What's it look like, love?'

'She's on fire,' I said, and started crying again.

Somebody put an arm round me and gave me a squeeze, and this time my brain decided to take a break.

Segments of the next hour or so remained in my memory: an ambulanceman holding a mask over my nose and mouth – doors slamming – a siren screaming – trolleys and lifts – lights on ceilings – pain that reared up and died down in one part of my body, and then ripped into it somewhere else. Bits scissored out of my consciousness like cuttings for a scrapbook. Weeks later I heard, as if I was saying it, 'Where's Daisy?'

'Daisy who?'

My eyelids felt like raw pork but I got them open wide enough to see Plod. When I opened them again she'd metamorphosed into Sue.

'Daisy,' I said. My throat felt as if somebody had reemed it with a wire brush.

'She's alright. I've got her.'

I heard somebody whimpering, but my eyes hurt so I shut them again.

Plod

The next time Plod appeared at my bedside I was not at my best. I felt vulnerable enough meeting my ex's new lover while in a hospital bed. With a bedpan jammed under me I felt totally disadvantaged.

'Who let you in?' I croaked, reaching for the call switch.

'Is it inconvenient?' she asked.

'You could say that.'

The nurse was apologetic and ticked Plod off, sending her out of the room while the bedpan was removed.

'I'll have to let her back in – doctor says you're fit enough to be interviewed.'

I looked at my bandaged hands and the sling on my left arm. 'A lot he knows,' I said, but the nurse had gone.

Plod returned. 'Is it alright if I sit down?' She did anyway, got a notebook out of her bag and clicked her ballpoint. 'I'd like to hear what happened. Take your time, in your own words.' The pen hovered.

'Dear sir, re your hide in which I was very nearly burnt to a crisp on the something inst, colon, I wish to complain about the quality of the wood.'

The pen began an upwards movement away from the notebook. 'It burns far too quickly and, comma, in my opinion constitutes a serious hazard to innocent bird watchers, full stop.'

Plod sighed and regarded me with feigned tolerance. 'I know this is difficult – it is for me, too. I have to be here, so let's make it easy on both of us and then I can leave you in peace.'

'Where's Sue?'

'Outside as a matter of fact – and very worried about you.'

'How touching.'

Plod's air of professional detachment became a little ruffled, and I knew she wanted to make some stinging reply, but all she said was 'You'll have to talk to us sooner or later' and shut the notebook. She looked very smart, very power-dressed, as she walked to the door in her black court shoes and long black trench coat. 'I'll be outside. Perhaps Sue can get you to see sense.'

Sue was a picture of anxiety, which gave me a certain amount of pleasure that was both sadistic and self-pitying. She almost kissed my cheek, but thought better of it.

'Am I that ugly?' I said tersely.

She shook her head, looking hurt. 'I didn't think you wanted me to.'

'I don't. I just want to know how Daisy is.'

'Missing you and still a bit nervous –'

'Just like you.'

An almost undetectable tremor of her upper lip made me relent. I'd spent my small reserve of energy on baiting Plod and was beginning to feel spaced out.

'It must be the stuff they give me – I don't know what I'm talking about half the time,' I told her.

Sue's voice was a bit feathery, but I was relieved she was back in control. 'I'm supposed to get you to talk to the police. If you won't talk to Viv she'll get someone else.'

Viv, eh?

'Mig, where's Jack?'

'In Belgium, with Mark – but I don't want them told. By the time he gets back I'll be out of here and he needn't be any the wiser.'

I caught her you-must-be-kidding look and wondered if I was in a worse state than I'd imagined.

'How long have I been here?' I asked her.

'Since yesterday morning, early.

There was something important I'd meant to do on Monday. I was scratching around in my brain for what it was when Sue said 'You realise you'll probably have to foot the bill for the hide if it was your fault.'

Bill! That was it – I was going to take the photographs to Bill Fletcher. Except that there weren't any photographs any more.

'Where are my things?' I asked, interrupting whatever it was Sue was saying.

'Your clothes, you mean? What's left of them I've taken home to get cleaned. Your wax jacket and walking boots are ruined – they probably protected you from worse burns that you've got.' She leant forward and held my arm gently. 'Mig, was it an accident?'

'Probably, I can't remember.'

She let go and and sat back, obviously unconvinced. 'Then what about the broken collar bone and the bruise on your mouth?'

'I fell over. Didn't they find anything else of mine outside the hide – or in it?'

'An empty liqueur bottle,' said Sue, disapprovingly. 'And your binoculars, all melted. And the remains of a can of petrol – what did you take petrol with you for?'

'In case I ran out of Benedictine.'

Sensibly, she ignored me. 'You didn't really go bird-watching in the dark, did you?'

I think she feared for my sanity. Maybe she thought our break-up had pushed me over the edge.

Instead of disabusing her of the idea, I asked what she'd done with my jacket.

'Thrown it in the dustbin.'

I groaned. Somewhere in the murky recesses of my mind was the image of me thrusting a partially-burnt photograph into my pocket. Perhaps I dreamt it.

'Is this what you're worried about?'

I opened my eyes. On the white NHS sheet, in glorious Kodakcolour fading into sepia and charcoal, was Dulcie – and Mandy, Catterell and somebody else. The rest had been erased.

We both sat staring at it, me with a mixture of relief and regret, as usual, and Sue – I could only guess what she was thinking, and before she could put it into words, I said 'Have you shown this to anyone?' meaning Plod.

'Hardly.'

'Thank god for that.'

'You can trust her, you know,' said Sue. 'If this has got anything to do with the fire you ought to tell her.'

I laughed. 'Yes, it would look good, wouldn't it! She could do me for pyromania *and* pornography. Help me pick this damn thing up.'

Sue fingered the picture as if it was covered in excrement, the corners of her mouth turned down with distate. 'What am I supposed to do with it?'

'You'll have to take it back with you,' I told her. 'I haven't got anywhere to put it, have I?'

Reluctantly she put it back into her shoulder bag.

'Is there a mirror in there?' She held it up in front of me. 'I never did like my eyebrows,' I said. 'And my hair needed trimming anyway. Nobody to do it since you –'

Sue put an arm gingerly round my shoulders.

'If my lungs weren't kippered I'd say you were wearing Musk.'

'Pachouli,' she said. 'You bloody idiot.' Her voice was muffled in the remains of my hair. 'You could have died.'

I patted her back clumsily with wadded hands. 'Tell Plod it was an accident. Get her off my back.'

Sue drew back. 'Plod?'

'Viv – Pc Plod – her outside.'

'I can't – and she's not a Pc, she's a Dc. You'll still have to make a statement, whether it's to her or someone else.'

'But not today. I'm shattered. You can persuade her to put it off until I'm up to it, can't you?'

Sue looked doubtful, but she did it, gaining me a day in which to either make up a story – or share my secrets with the very people I feared had some of the best reasons for hushing them up.

Visitors

Gill, Rachel and Ellie called in that evening. Sue had told them where I was and they'd tried to phone Maureen to tell her, but she wasn't home. I told them where she was, but not why. Catterell wouldn't be bothered about my friends now he thought he'd destroyed all the pictures and, if my suspicions about the police were right, he'd soon be told about my reluctance to make a statement. He'd take that as a sign that I was either afraid of him and what he'd do – which wasn't entirely untrue – or that I realised without evidence I wouldn't have much of a story to tell.

My friends didn't stay long. My barbecued bits were giving me gip and Gill went and found the Staff Nurse who came immediately like a Fairy Godmother with a wand that magicked me into morphined bliss. As I slid away into painless silence I thought of Mandy dumped by the sewage outflow.

The Staff Nurse re-appeared the next morning while my dressings were being changed. The hands weren't as bad as I thought and I wanted to know when she was going to let me out.

'Another couple of days won't do any harm – don't you like it here?'

'Hospitals aren't my favourite places,' I said, apologetically.

She beamed at me through her glasses: 'Nor mine, but don't tell anybody. I especially don't like having the police bothering patients. Are you up to seeing them today?'

I'd thought of little else since being woken with a cup of tea while it was still dark, and I'd decided that Plod might be the answer to my dilemma. She was a woman, after all.

'Wheel her in,' I said. 'It's not a her – it's a him.'

Him was a different kettle of detective from her. For a start he was a Det.Sgt, a scrawny moustachioed man with little brown eyes like frozen Maltesers, who hadn't the time or the sensitivity to put up with any nonsense from self-immolating women.

'Where's the woman who was here yesterday?' I asked.

'Dc Jackson has been reassigned. Now let's get on with this, shall we.' It was a demand, not a question. 'What were you doing at the nature reserve on Sunday night?'

'Bird watching?'

The impenetrable eyes regarded me hard for a mere

second and then dropped as he wrote something in his notebook.

'How did the fire start?'

'Somebody threw a can of patrol into the hide.'

The eyes shot up. 'Did you see who it was?'

Whatever I told him it wouldn't matter, so long as it wasn't the truth. He was either there because he didn't give a damn one way or the other, or because he knew. He was just going through the motions. 'No.'

The eyes didn't look up again until the interview was over. 'Did you break into the hut?'

'No.'

'Why would anyone throw petrol? Did they know you were in there?'

'Vandals?' I suggested.

'How did you come by your injuries?'

'I fell over trying to get out of the hut in a panic.'

'And you didn't see anyone – running away, or before the fire? And you were bird-watching – in the dark?'

'Have you finished?'

He had. 'There may be further enquiries, Miss Hills. You're not leaving the area when the hospital releases you?'

'Oh yes, I'm spending the rest of the winter in the Bahamas. Sunbathing,' I added, waving my hands at him. He wasn't moved.

'That's alright then. We'll be in touch.'

'Do that. I'll be fascinated to hear the outcome.'

He shut the notebook with a snap and bunged it into his inside pocket next to whatever organ substituted for a heart. 'You were a very lucky woman – there's some nasty types about. Stay where you belong in future. It's asking for trouble wandering about at night in out-of-the-way places.'

'Especially if you're a woman,' I said, just to see how he'd react. The Maltesers didn't thaw for a moment.

'That's the way it is. Just remember that.'

For a long time after he'd gone I sat looking out of the window at seagulls grazing in the field behind the hospital, their beaks into the wind. Had he been sent to warn me, or was it just the good advice of a practical man?

120

Sue came that evening, bringing my laundered clothing in a big carrier bag.

She hadn't known that Plod had been taken off the case: 'She won't like that,' she said.

It was on the tip of my tongue to say 'Know her that well, do you?' but I bit it back. If Plod had been deliberately removed she couldn't be involved and there was still the possibility that she could be an ally. Besides, I was enjoying Sue's sympathy and attention.

She hadn't mentioned the photograph, which I thought was exemplary self-restraint on her part – if Sue had nearly been incinerated clutching an obscene picture I'd have wanted to know what was going on.

'Did the police give you a hard time?' she was asking.

It was a perfectly logical question, given my weird attitude towards making any sort of statement.

'How do you mean?'

'Why do you keep answering questions with more questions?'

'Because the answers, Horatio, create problems beyond your understanding.'

It always irritated Sue if I said things she didn't understand, even when I did it unintentionally. It did now. And really she deserved better. So it all came out in a gout that she couldn't begin to fully take in, and at the end of it, as I dwindled off, she looked as if she could hit me.

'And that's about it,' I said.

She started walking round the bed, which was a strain on my neck. 'Stand still, you're making me dizzy.'

'Making *you* dizzy! You tell me you're involved in a porn ring – women have been murdered – that somebody tried to murder you – that the police might be involved –'

'And you don't believe me?'

She stopped circling and jammed her hands onto the bed, making me jump. 'Of course I believe you, you silly bitch! And don't look at me like that – I might be a feminist, but there are times when – you're the fucking limit! Why didn't you tell me sooner?'

'You didn't seem interested,' I said, pathetically.

'Oh my god!' She clamped her hands to her temples. 'Is

this what it's all about – Viv? There's nothing going on with us, you . . . twit!'

I sank back against the pillows, images of me and Maureen scouring my mind. 'Does this mean . . . ?'

'What?' But she knew what I meant. 'I don't know – let's get this sorted out first.' I felt disappointed. Our relationship mightn't be ideal but it was the only one I'd got. 'Look,' I said, 'I'm really knackered. Can we continue this tomorrow?'

But Sue was adamant: 'You're not going to put me off again. I want to know what you're going to do about this hostel business. You've still got one photo left – isn't that enough evidence?'

'All it tells anybody is that Catterell plays roles in sex games. And if I give it to the police it could get conveniently lost.'

'Viv wouldn't do anything like that!' Sue protested. 'Let me show it to her and see what she thinks.'

I had a lot of misgivings – about Sue getting involved, about Plod's ability to do anything – but I agreed, making Sue promise not to let the photograph go. Sue was getting enthusiastic about nailing Catterell, and that worried me. Conscience may make coward's of most people, but in my case it was imagination, and if there was any way I could slide under the door instead of booting it in, I'd rather find it. Subtlety had never been Sue's strong point: if something needed saying or doing, she said and did it. I realised she was finding this whole thing energising, which wasn't surprising – it was the antidote to my lethargy.

'I'll be back tomorrow, after I've talked to Viv,' she said, planting a kiss on my face. 'They shouldn't get away with this.' I basked in her protectiveness, for a moment. 'Poor Daisy is a nervous wreck – she's got a bump the size of an egg on her head and a singed coat. The bastards!'

I wasn't entitled to any goodies off the drug trolley that night, so I lay awake listening to the usual hospital din and remembering back to when I'd last been here . . . Mark had gone to Europe, having failed to persuade me to have an abortion. He hadn't 'deserted' me, as they say – our relationship was over before I got pregnant, but it had dragged on as these things tend to do. The pregnancy was catalytic, freeing us both to decide what it was we wanted, which in Mark's case was not competition. I didn't blame him. And I didn't tell him that I'd deliberately got pregnant because that was what I wanted. Wanted more than him. After that I just got tired of men. They had said it all and done it all and they didn't seem to be going anywhere. We were still hearing the tired old arguments about why women weren't 'up' there with them, could never be because our innards didn't dangle between our legs or our hormones were out of control or whatever.

Cautiously I flexed my fingers inside the bandaging. Men used to burn women who got in their way. So what was new?

Home sweet home

I discharged myself, not out of bravado but because the Fairy Godmother wanted to change my pumpkin from the security of a private room.

'I need the bed,' she said apologetically and then, confidentially, 'for a wealthy Kuwaiti.'

I tried ringing Sue, but she must have been at work, so I got a taxi home. The house was an even bigger mess. This time they'd done a more thorough job, slinging stuff over the floors and breaking things. They'd even taken the video, I suppose to make it look like an ordinary burglary. Jack's room didn't look much untidier than usual, but even there you could detect their efforts where they'd gone through his music tapes and videos, the only things he ever kept in order. I tried cleaning up, but it was difficult with the bandaged hands and trussed arm.

The video rental people weren't happy about the theft even though I assured them I was insured; and Jack wasn't happy when I phoned Brussels. I let the phone ring for some minutes before a sleepy, grumpy voice said 'Lo.'

'That sounds like a lot of late nights.' I tried to sound bright.

'Mum?'

123

'Who else? How are you getting on over there?'

'S'alright.'

'Getting on with Mark?'

'S'pose so. Mum, I was asleep! What d'you want?'

'Nothing. Just checking. Thought you might miss my scintillating company.'

'Yeah. Bye.'

'Jack – I love you.'

'Yeah. Me too. 'Night.'

It was 10.30 in the morning. I let him go and rang Maureen's number. She didn't let me off so lightly, but then I didn't expect her to. She was angry, confused and frightened. I'd done a good job unsettling her, crumbling some of the security she'd taken a couple of years rebuilding. She'd allowed someone a small step into her life and the result was this.

'Somebody's been watching me – he was there when I left the flat, he's outside my parent's house. I can see him now, sitting in a car. Is it something to do with you? Because if it is I want it stopped. Do you understand?'

'He's a friend,' I told her. 'I asked him to hang around.'

'This has got something to do with what's in the paper today, hasn't it.'

I hadn't seen the paper, but it was obvious that there'd be a report on the fire. I'd just forgotten. 'It's nothing to worry about,' I said. 'I'll explain, but not over the phone – it's too complicated.'

'What about Sue?' Maureen persisted. 'You said it had something to do with her.'

'I was wrong. Maureen, don't worry. I over-reacted the other day. You're quite safe. Believe me.'

I wouldn't have blamed her if she never believed anything I said again, but I didn't want her to hate me.

As soon as I got off the phone I rang Danny to tell him to call off his watchdog, then left a message for Sue at the vet's to say I was home. Then I went out to buy a pair of Marigolds and a paper. I'd made the front page.

WOMAN HURT IN THUGS' FIRE BOMB ATTACK
(At least that bit was true)

Police are keeping secret the identity of a woman
who narrowly escaped death in a bizarre and vicious

124

arson attack on a bird watchers hide at the Marshland nature reserve on Sunday night.

The woman is believed to have been keeping a nature watch vigil inside the all-wooden hut when vandals, who had previously broken into the building, returned and flung a petrol can and some sort of incendiary through the door.

'We don't know whether they knew somebody was inside the hide,' said Insp. Derek Makin yesterday. 'It's difficult to believe anyone could deliberately endanger the life of an innocent person, but we have to look into all the possibilities.'

The fire brigade was alerted at about 11.45pm by Mrs Billy Dawson, landlady of the nearby Gun and Hunter pub, who spotted the blaze as she was letting her dog out into the garden before locking up for the night.

Two fire engines attended but the hide was destroyed, causing an estimated £2,000 damage.

The unnamed woman was taken to hospital by ambulance where she is said to be 'comfortable'.

'We're not revealing her identity for fear of possible reprisals,' said Insp. Makin. 'I would urge anybody – and especially women – not to go alone on night-time activities of this kind, particularly in out-of-the-way places.

'There's been a lot of vandalism at the nature reserve over the last few months, which is one of the reasons why the gates are shut at dusk.

'Strictly speaking this woman shouldn't have been on the property and she is extremely lucky to be alive today.'

So that was the official line: nobody was warning bait-diggers not to frequent the bay 'out of hours' – just women who were asking for trouble if they strayed once night had fallen. Neat.

I pulled one of the bubblegum-pink Marigolds over the bandages on my right hand and poured lukewarm water in a bowl. While I was waiting for Sue to get in touch I laboriously cleaned the kitchen. It needed it but that wasn't why I did it: I was tidying up a small area of my life to make myself feel better.

Plod blown

Sue came round at lunch-time and I knew from the way she looked that she hadn't got any good news.

'Why've you left hospital?' she demanded before she'd got through the front door.

'Welcome home, Mig, all is forgiven.'

'Don't be pathetic.' She shut the door and tugged my arm as I walked away from her. 'Give us a hug.'

We hugged. 'Bad news?' I asked.

'She won't touch it.'

'I'm not surprised,' I said, leading the way into the living-room. 'In her position, neither would I.'

'What's that supposed to mean?' Sue sounded angry and defeated.

'What did she say when you showed her the photograph?'

'She said she'd put out feelers and nobody wanted to know. And then she was taken to one side and told she was asking for trouble. She's really worried now – I've never seen her like that. I think she thinks she's damaged her career.'

I allowed myself a quick fantasy image of a disconcerted Plod, which was gratifying because I wasn't sure Sue hadn't lied about their relationship. I didn't mind the lie – it meant she cared enough about us not to risk permanent damage. Besides, it made me feel less badly about Maureen.

Sue rolled me a cigarette. 'She did say one thing – that man in the picture – not Catterell, the other one – is a copper, a 'big' one she said.'

'Who?'

Sue laughed drily. 'She wouldn't tell me, but the way she reacted he must be one of the Untouchables.'

Danny had been right. 'Don't be too hard on her,' I said. 'She's the wrong rank and the wrong sex to take on a crooked Establishment. It must be difficult at the best of times for a woman in a male network. I imagine you either go with them or they gang up on you. Her life would be hell unless she could find some sea-green incorruptible in a high enough position.'

'All the same –'

I could afford to be generous, and secretly a bit smug: 'Would you risk your career because you knew one man was taking part in porny parties? We don't even know if he knew he was being filmed, or that the woman in it had a history of mental illness and didn't want to take part. He might have thought Dulcie was just playing a role. He wouldn't be the first policeman to to go in for that sort of thing – and I wouldn't mind betting there'd be a lot of unofficial sympathy from 'the lads' if he got caught at it.'

'But if I knew people had been murdered because of it I'd have to do something,' Sue persisted.

'Even if it meant being exposed as a lesbian?'

'There're hundreds of lesbians in the Police! Some of the male officers know about Viv, but they don't make a big deal about it – well, sly digs and stuff like that maybe, but they don't threaten her because of it.'

'Remember Annie?' I said. 'She got thrown out of the Army and it nearly destroyed her. She loved that job but it didn't make any difference. Come on Sue! – it didn't even matter that the officers who chucked her out included dykes!'

'I suppose you're right,' Sue sighed. All the same, she was disappointed and disillusioned and I knew Plod had blown it. 'What are we going to do then – just forget it?'

I shrugged my right shoulder. 'Just now I haven't a clue. Catterell's way ahead of me – he's had more practice and he's got some powerful friends. It's not just this policeman – there's a struck-off doctor who used to be part of an international child-abuse racket, and a couple of heavies who could be drug-dealers or coppers – or both for all I know! All I've got on my side is a small-time pusher who's on probation and for whom I feel responsible. Besides, there's Jack – he'll be back soon and I can't put him at risk. I had this great idea of getting it all sorted before he returned. How naive can you get? And then there's you – they're bound to know about you by now.'

'Don't worry about me.' Sue was endearingly fierce at times.

She had to go back to work but she promised to come back later with Daisy who'd been checked over by the vet and given some mild tranquillisers.

'Get some for me, will you?' I was only half-joking.

Sue hadn't been gone ten minutes when the phone rang. I'd have ignored it in case it was Catterell, but then it might have been Jack or Mark.

It was Dorothy. Unwin wanted an interview and she'd volunteered. 'Just tell me no comment and I'll be pleased to pass on the message.' I thanked her for her protection. 'What are friends for? Anyway, I like to spoil his day – it makes mine.'

It occurred to me that my identity was supposed to have been kept quiet. 'Unwin's pally with the police – I expect they belong to the same Lodge,' she said. 'Anyway, he doesn't know who you are which is why I thought it best if I handled it. He's got one or two arse-lickers on the staff and you don't want them bothering you. Are you alright by the way? If there's anything I can do . . . '

Well, what were friends for?

'You remember that Dr Cockburn – is his sister still around?'

She was as far as Dorothy knew. 'She dropped out of the Twinning Association after that business with her brother and the last I heard she was doing good works at St Luke's with down-and-outs. Her name's Lampert or Lambert, something like that.' Dorothy didn't ask any questions but I sensed that her professional interest, despite the blunting effect of too many years in the business, was aroused. I trusted her enough to tell her there was one hell of a story in the offing but that it would take the muscle of Fleet Street to dig it out.

'Are you interested?' Catterell might have friends in high places, but they couldn't hide forever from the relentless probing of a national newspaper with infinite resources and fat cheque books.

'I don't know,' said Dorothy cautiously. She didn't need the hassle or the money, and I couldn't give her anything yet that would convince a news editor it was worth starting what might be a lengthy and expensive inquiry. And if Catterell suspected that I had blown the whistle. . . .

'I can't tell you much because I haven't got enough to go on,' I admitted. 'But when I do you'll be the first to know.'

'Well, mind how you go – you seem to be disturbing

some pretty vicious hornets' nests these days. Next time you might not be so lucky.'

'Oh I'm really lucky,' I said. 'I've got a broken collar bone, grilled fingers, no eyebrows and a half-bald dog having a nervous breakdown. Apart from that life's wonderful.'

Dorothy wouldn't join in the joke. 'Unless you've a very good reason for poking your nose in, my advice is – don't.'

It was good advice and I did take it seriously. I actually sat down and made a list of reasons for and against going on:

FOR	AGAINST
Dulcie's murder	Risk to Jack
Mandy's murder	ditto me
Sid's murder	maybe Sue
Exploitation of the vulnerable	
Pornographizing women	
Burglary	
Intimidation	
Attempted murder of me	
ditto Daisy	
Corrupt policemen	

There were probably things I'd forgotten, but as I fumbled about trying to do ordinary jobs with one arm in a sling – like take a shower, wash up, prepare food – my resentment grew until I caught myself muttering threats to an absent enemy as I wrestled with a piece of wood I was trying to chop one-handed. I was on my knees in the backyard trying to hold it with my left hand without disturbing the collar bone or hacking off my finger tips. Instinctively I was letting go just before the hatchet made contact, and the wood was leaping about all over the place. I was getting verbally very graphic when I became aware that old Mrs Next door Left was regarding me over the garden wall.

'You mind you don't cut yourself. They're nasty, dangerous things, choppers.'

You can say that again, I thought.

'Had a little accident, have you? You need a man to do that for you. They're used to that sort of thing. I wish my hubby was alive – he used to do all the jobs like that.' She gave a brave little sigh which turned into a chuckle. 'We can't live with them and we can't live without them, can we.'

'I can,' I said, and brought the hatchet down on the concrete.

She went away with an armful of perfectly-laundered drawers and nighties. My washing line always looked like an advert for the soap powder that dozy, uncaring mums used. Mrs Next door Right even washed her yellow dusters, and Mrs Next door Left actually washed the washing line. Face it, I thought, you're a slob.

Friends

Even if I hadn't made the list with its disproportionate FOR column, my mind would have been made up at the sight of Daisy: when Sue brought her home she slunk into the house, naked tail between her featherless legs, and an expression in her eyes that said 'Don't hit me.'

Sue diplomatically left us alone and went into the kitchen with the Indian take-away she'd bought. When I put my arm round the dog she was all of a tremble, but her fat grey tail made a couple of thumps on the floor, and she took advantage of the situation to climb up on the sofa next to me. Her paws and head drooped over the side but she kept her eyes cocked up at me to make sure she wasn't dreaming.

We'd eaten the Indian and I was looking forward to an evening of mindless telly-watching when somebody rapped on the front door (I don't like bells or chimes). Daisy, who normally launched herself into the hall in a froth, stayed put in front of the fire.

'Shall I go?' said Sue.

I shook my head. 'Let's have a look first.'

We crept down the hall and I stuck my eye to the spy-hole.

It was Gill and Ellie – and Maureen.

For the next ten minutes I was on tenterhooks wondering what Maureen was going to say in front of Sue. I should have known better. Maureen had obviously initiated the visit but hadn't told Gill or Ellie what had happened between her and me. And if the others suspected anything, they were keeping it to themselves.

'We've come to help,' said Gill. 'And we want to know what's going on.'

So I told them.

Sue said it was the second sensible thing I'd done for a long time; Gill had a go at me for not telling them sooner; Ellie just sat shaking her head, her eyes huge with disbelieve; and Maureen remained diplomatically silent.

'So what do we do?' said Gill finally.

'Get the bastards!' said Ellie, her eyes gleaming.

'How?' said Maureen, quietly.

'Go in there and sort this Catterell out,' said Sue.

'I' had become 'we'. It was a nice feeling which didn't last long when I thought about the risk to them and their children.

Ellie pointed out that she didn't have any kids and that she was 'between' jobs so her time was at my disposal. I accepted Gill's offer to drive me about, provided she stayed out of sight if we decided to pay Catterell a visit. Sue was working but she didn't want to be excluded – 'We've got some really sharp scalpels at work – I could think of one or two things to do with them.' Maureen didn't offer and I didn't ask.

Sue stayed the night, insisting that I couldn't manage on my own.

'I'll sleep in Jack's room if you prefer,' she offered.

It made sense, but I felt the need of somebody warm and human in bed next to me. When she helped me undress we were both awkward, but the icy sheets drove us into a huddle and we started small-talking the way you do in the dark. I've never known anyone drop off so suddenly as Sue does: one minute she's talking and the next she's gone. Her breathing gradually turned into a gentle snore and I prepared myself for a night of broken sleep. I couldn't remember where I'd got to with the list, so I started at A again: Jane Austen, Nina Auerbach, Abigail Adams . . . Eleanor Butler, Fanny Burney, Simone de Beauvoir. . .

Daisy was making funny noises on the landing, so against my better judgement I let her in. While she cleaned the parts of herself that required the most slurping and nibbling and Sue's snoring reached the pneumatic drill level, I tried to get comfortable and think about my next move. When I eventually slept I dreamt I was lying on a beach. The tide was coming in and leaving me covered with a flotsam of panti liners and human faeces. Some men were fishing behind me, casting reels of film over my body into the filthy water. 'It's coming from Belgium,' one of them said, but nobody tried to move me and I couldn't because I was supposed to be sleeping. A bloated black shape floated inshore and I tried to scramble up the sand away from it. As it rolled onto me it turned out to be Mandy in her bomber jacket. 'More human sewage,' somebody said.

In the dream I was screaming my lungs out, but the noise that woke me was a strangled mewing from the back of my throat.

Sisterhood

Gill picked me up at 9.30 the next morning and drove over to Ellie's. She emerged laden with cameras.

'Nervous?' I asked.

'Bloody terrified. Let's go for it.'

We left Gill parked a street away and walked to St Luke's, a gleaming flint Gothic monstrosity rearing above the surrounding shops and houses and not three minutes' walk from the Sea Chalet. Next to it, almost as an afterthought, was the parish hall in pink brick. I dug my old Press card out of my pocket and we went in.

It doesn't matter where you go in England – and, for all I know, anywhere else – church halls share a common identity, that smell of gas and tea urns, homemade cakes and stale jumble sales.

Even at 10 o'clock in the morning there were several tramps and bag ladies sitting at the paste tables dipping bread into steaming mugs.

'Can I help you?' This had to be the Reverend Tony Lester, beaming, energetic, in denims and dog collar. I remembered him from the old days, and guessed he wouldn't remember me.

'Jane Liddell,' I said, hoping it was a sufficiently unmemorable name. 'I'm a freelance journalist and I wondered whether you'd mind me doing a feature on the work you do here.'

It wasn't totally untrue – I could knock up something for the rag.

'Delighted,' he said. 'We need all the publicity we can get – good publicity, that is.'

I assured him that was my intention and he spent the next half an hour describing the problems of running a service for commercially unattractive human beings in a seaside town. 'The hoteliers would rather we went somewhere else – it's their living they're worried about, you see. They even called in the local MP to see how the area is "being spoiled" by the presence on the streets of what one of them called "parasites".'

'What sort of people come to St Luke's?' I asked.

'It's not just the homeless, although God knows there's enough of them. We get women from the B and Bs who can't feed their children, young people who've left home and aren't entitled to the dole but can't get work – this area has the highest level of unemployment in the county. You knew? Of course.'

'What about the Community Care system?'

The Rector let out a very unclerical snort: 'That's a mixed bag, if you like. The caring services do a wonderful job with limited resources, but the truth is that a lot of these people simply can't cope in the community. I have one lad who comes here every day; schizophrenic, violent, and his 67 year old mother is supposed to look after him! He wants to go back, but until he does something wrong he's got to stay on the outside. They're not all like that, of course. Lots of them don't need a soup kitchen so much as a place to go where somebody is interested in them. We have socials. things like that that they enjoy.'

I wondered whether Dulcie had ever been here and how I could introduce her name into the conversation. 'Anybody from the hostels around here? – I used to know a woman who lived at a place called the Chalet, or something –'

'Dulcie! is that the one? Now there was a character – she used to sing for us. Said she was in films.'

But not what sort. 'You cater for all religions then? You don't mind Catholics?'

Lester laughed good-naturedly: 'We don't discriminate. Why d'you ask?'

'I thought Dulcie was a Catholic,' I told him, thinking back to her reference to the Pope.

'Not as far as I know. As a matter of fact, she was one of my parishioners. Came to services regularly. You know what happened to her, don't you? Quite dreadful. We were all very upset. I knew she'd had problems, but I was shocked all the same.'

I was dying to ask him what sort of problems. Instead I said 'She was going to be married, the last time I saw her.'

Lester shook his head sadly. 'I know. I'd met her fiancé – nice old chap.'

Ellie took pictures of the Rector, the women helpers in the kitchen and one or two of the customers who didn't 'object'.

I asked Lester if there were any more volunteers.

'Quite a few, but they're not all here on the same day. There's Mrs.Lambert, of course. I don't know what we'd do without Celia. She's our organisational genius. Come over to the office and I'll introduce you.'

Celia Lambert bore little resemblance to her brother. I remembered him as pale and corpulent, whereas she was brown and diminutive. Her manner was efficient and brusque almost to the point of rudeness, but Lester didn't seem to notice, probably couldn't afford to. He introduced us and then left to sort out one of his many problems.

Mrs Lambert regarded me with intelligent, guarded eyes. It was difficult to decide her age – she could have been anywhere between 55 and 65, but beneath the expensive woollens there was, I suspected, a hard, fit body. I had her down for a tennis and bridge player. She didn't want her picture taken, and she didn't want to be quoted directly. 'I'm backroom stuff and that's the way I like it. I don't want publicity, but I'll fill in the details for you. What do you want to know?'

This was it. I could feel Ellie tensed up beside me in the small room. Celia Lambert's eyes took on a puzzled, apprehensive look just before they hardened with suspicion.

'What is it you want?' she demanded.

'We're not the gutter Press, Mrs.Lambert,' I said quickly, panicking. 'I haven't come here to drag your name into print again if that's what you're thinking – '

I was making a right hash of it. She started to stand up.

'But I do need something – your help,' I added as she came round the desk. She pushed past me and headed for the door to throw us out. 'It's about your brother.'

Mrs Lambert pulled the door open angrily and held it, waiting for us to leave.

'We could discuss it in front of everybody out there, but I think you'd rather keep it private,' I blathered. 'That's the way it will stay.'

The hardened journo pose didn't fool her for a moment. 'Get out,' she said, as if she was used to saying it and used to being obeyed.

'We're not the Press, Mrs Lambert,' I tried. She didn't move. 'Two women have died because of something your brother may be involved in – I don't know to what extent. I know you've suffered in the past, but you may be our only hope of ending a nasty racket right here on your own doorstep.'

It didn't budge her an inch, but I thought I detected a small element of doubt in those hostile eyes. I could have been wrong. I sighed: 'Okay Mrs Lambert, we're going.' I leant over her desk and scribbled my phone number on her notepad. 'If you change your mind you can reach me here.'

She refused to take the slip of paper so I put it back on the desk. As we left I said 'I'd appreciate it if you didn't show that to anybody else – or mention my visit. The people your brother mixes with play rough, as you can see.'

Outside Ellie let out a long sigh as if she'd been holding her breath. 'That was dreadful. Is that how you used to earning a living?'

'Don't worry – I wasn't much good at it then, either. What would it take to move that woman? She's as tough as old boots.'

'My hands are still shaking,' said Ellie, holding them up for me to see. 'I doubt if I could have taken her picture anyway. Do you think she'll get in touch?'

'It's who with I'm worried about.'

I was still thinking about the possibilities when we got back to the Volvo.

'Where to now?' asked Gill after Ellie had told her about our brief encounter with Cockburn's sister.

I got her to drive over to the Probation Office. Bill Fletcher was in 'but busy'.

'It's urgent,' I told the receptionist. She was reluctant to bother him because he was in conference. I was getting tired of failing: 'Just tell him I'm here and it's important. It won't wait – and neither will I.'

Peeved, she pulled her fist-proof window shut and got on the phone. She took her time having a chat with somebody who I bet had nothing to do with Bill, and then, when she was good and ready, slid the window open. 'You can go up,' she said, and slammed it shut again. Bill met me on the stairs. 'Mig, I'm really sorry, but I actually am in conference. What's up?'

I showed him the photograph. 'Recognise anyone?'

'Bloody hell!' he said, running his hand through his hair.

'Recognise any of the men?'

'Isn't that Jimmy Catterell?'

'Anybody else?'

He shook his head. 'Only little Mandy. Christ, Mig, what's going on?'

'Got an hour or so to spare?'

'Shit! Look, can you come back? – no, that's no good.

I've got court in an hour, and then I'm taking a lad to Norfolk.'

'It'll keep,' I said. 'But if you've any probationers working at the Sea Chalet you ought to think about getting them out. Just do it subtly – I'm in enough trouble as it is.'

'I can see that,' he said, indicating my arm and hands. 'I'll have to call in the police.'

'Not yet. Promise me, Bill. I've already been threatened and I've got a son to think about.'

One of his colleagues appeared at the top of the stairs: 'Richard's got to go in a few minutes. Can you make it snappy?'

'Coming,' said Bill, and turned back to me. 'As soon as I get back tomorrow, right?'

'Right.' He was halfway up the stairs in his hurry to get back to his meeting. 'Bill – the photograph?'

'Oh Christ! Here, take it. What a bloody mess!'

Before I'd got to the bottom of the stairs he stuck his head over the bannister: 'Mig, you take care.'

'You too,' I said.

It was the last time I saw him.

Food for thought

We had one more errand before we called it a day. Gill drove to the reserve so that Ellie could drive my car home. Only it wasn't there.

'Maybe the police moved it,' Gill suggested. 'For safe-keeping.'

Or maybe to search it – or stick a bug in it or –

'Let's go and have a drink,' I said, fed up with creeping paranoia.

The Gun and Hunter was quiet at that time of the day and Billy Dawson had plenty of time to chat. I asked her if she'd seen the police towing a blue Ford saloon away from the old garage on the night of the fire. She looked at my arm and sussed me out immediately.

'I've got it, love, in the rear car park. The police were just going to leave it there, by the road, but the side window had been smashed and I said bring it over here. Can you imagine? There wouldn't have been a tyre left on it! Or your radio would've been ripped out – on top of what happened to you! I don't know why we pay taxes sometimes. Thanks love – I'll have a bob's worth.'

She drew two quid's worth of gin off an optic without even turning round to look at it, and charged me 50p.

'Good health – and let's hope they catch the buggers who did that to you. I walk my dog out there. If I catch them they'll know it.'

I didn't doubt it. Billy was mouthy, brassy and hard – what she liked to think of as a no-nonsense landlady; she'd hang 'em and flog 'em, chuck out the foreigners, especially the blacks, bomb the IRA, and put Licensed Victuallers in Parliament. She was an ignorant woman and despite that I liked her.

Beside the optics that she handled so skilfully was a half-full card of peanut packets. Each packet torn from the card exposed another bit of a woman's body. So far the customers had paid to see one breast. Dulcie's had begun to succumb to gravity, but Mandy . . . 'Good pair of tits, Mandy' was what Catterell had said. For a small woman she'd had a big chest. Why was there only one photograph of her? Women with women – and yet in the picture she wasn't doing anything with Dulcie. She was just standing beside her. I tried to remember how many shots were in the envelope Mandy'd given me. It couldn't have been more than nine, or ten. Had Dulcie been selective when she stole them, leaving out the psuedo-lesbian scenes? It didn't seem likely: it was a 'sin' they'd forced her to commit. Wouldn't she want those as much as the other pictures in her scheme to punish her tormenters?

A group of men in greasy dungarees came in, filling the bar with loud joshing voices and the smell of oil. One of them asked Billy what was on the menu.

'You come in here every Thursday and ask me the same thing, Mick, and you get the same answer – we don't cook on Thursdays. There's crisps, nuts or chocolate.'

'That's bird food! Alright, give us some peanuts.'

Billy tore off one of the packets, revealing half a breast. 'Make it two,' Mick leered.

'You bloody animal!' said one of the other men.

'Nothing wrong with that. She's got what it takes – which is more than I can say for you, you little wooftah.'

They all rolled about laughing and taking the mickey out of the second man. 'Get off!' he said, grinning. 'Go on then, Billy, let's have some bloody peanuts as well.'

Had Mandy's sexual identity been important to her? She'd been quick enough to deny being a 'lezzie' when I challenged her about her role in the photography sessions. If it meant that much to her . . . Had she hidden the remaining photographs, or destroyed them?

I thanked Billy again as we left.

'Any time, darling – but not under the same circumstances, eh? You were–'

'I know,' I said, 'very lucky.'

Sue

Ellie dropped me off before taking the car onto the nearest garage to get a replacement for the window that I assumed Catterell had smashed. I felt dog-tired, my shoulder ached, and I couldn't settle to the preparation I needed to do before term started. I walked Daisy round the block and treated her to a chewy bar in the ironmongers. She was twitchy with traffic at the best of times, but today she was even shying away from people, and when the ironmonger bent over to give her his usual pat, she skidded to one side as if he was going to hit her.

'She's never done that before,' he said. 'She been in the wars?'

'Poor old girl,' said his wife. 'Come on, have a biscuit.' Daisy took it in her soft mouth. 'There you are! She's alright – just gone off men.' Mrs Minty patted the dog's head. 'I know just how you feel, my lovely.'

I made excuses for Daisy's nerves and cast an eye over the row of long-handled axes with gleaming blades, thinking about what I'd like to do with one of them if ever I had Catterell at my mercy.

Sue got off work early and came in as I was wrestling with the firewood again.

'Go and sit down,' she said. 'I've seen enough blood for one day.'

While she was putting together one of her spicy vegetarian stews I tried to open a bottle of wine, but it got the better of me and she had to do that too.

'Is it alright if I have a bath?' she asked, pulling the cork with one swift, easy movement.

'You don't have to ask.' I sounded as tetchy as I felt, but she humoured me which made me feel stupid as well as useless. When she went upstairs I tried to get my mind round the preparation work, which made me even more frustrated, so I gave up and poured another glass of wine. I was worried about Celia Lambert: if she was angry enough at being dragged into yet another of her brother's sordid affairs she might tackle him, and then it would just be a matter of time before Catterell knew I was on his back again. And unless Bill Fletcher knew the right buttons to push pdq I'd be a sitting target.

I'd expected Celia to be resistant but over-estimated my ability to persuade her to help. Why should she? If I'd had the photographs and could have thrust them under her nose maybe it would have shocked her into doing something, but one burnt offering that didn't include Cockburn wasn't much use.

The plonk tasted sour but I drank it womanfully while I wondered how the hell I'd ever got myself involved in this mess. If I'd bothered to read Dulcie's notes when she gave them to me she might still be alive, and Catterell and the whole bunch of them might be behind bars. I got the photocopied notes out again and spread them on the floor around me. HELP ME screamed from the crumpled pages.

I fled upstairs, taking the bottle and two glasses with me.

Sue wanted to know what had happened during the day so I sat on the bath surround and told her.

'This is getting to you isn't it,' she said. 'You need to relax. Why don't you get in?'

Her wet hair was clinging to her neck, and her eyes had assumed that special depth which once upon a time I had gladly drowned in.

'What about the sling?' I asked, but I was already getting undressed.

'Switch off the light,' she said.

'She made room for me between her legs and folded her arms around me. Her breasts were warm and slippery against my back. In the steam and the red glow from the wall heater I watched her hands as she slid the hot silky water over my body. When she raised her knees under mine there was only the splash of water in the intense silence. An ugly image was gnawing at the edges of my mind as her hands glided down the inside of my thighs into the water, and I groaned, waiting for the sick stab of obscenity.

'It's alright.' Her mouth was speaking softly against my throat. Gently she turned my head and her mouth found mine, ssshing against my lips, tasting, kissing out the pain, while her fingers rose and dipped beneath the water.

The code broken

It was Sue who discovered the identity of the policeman. After dinner she'd begun reading Dulcie's notes.

'It's almost as if she's written them in code,' she said, holding her glasses up to the light as if they might be the reason she couldn't decipher Dulcie's handwriting. 'If J.C. isn't Jesus Christ but James Catterell, pp means what? – parish priest? The man you spoke to today?'

'Lester. Dulcie'd told him she was in films, but of course he didn't believe her. She can't have told him what sort of films or he'd have been bound to take her more seriously . . . I suppose. Would you necessarily believe a mentally-disturbed woman who thought the Post Office was trying to bugger you with invisible rays? If she'd gone on about stuff like that, Lester might not have taken her seriously, even then.

141

'It was the "pp" that made me think she was Catholic – that and her references to the Pope.'

'But she doesn't say *the* Pope. She says Pope. And if the priest wasn't a Catholic one and Pope doesn't have a watchermacallit in front –'

'A definite article –'

'Right, one of those. If it doesn't have that could it be somebody's name instead?'

We stared at one another. 'Like a policeman,' I said.

Sue returned to the notes: 'Look. she doesn't use definite article or words like "a" either. Does that mean they should be there, or that Pope didn't need a "the" anyway?'

'It's difficult to tell – her mind tended to leapfrog when she wrote. You can see how she goes from "J.C. cant make me or Pope if thats what he wants or pp Im not doing it anymore" to the apparently unrelated fact that she bought "Crime and Punishment" that day.'

'Yes, but they're not unrelated, are they. She wants Dovstoyevsky to help her presumably because he wrote a book with a title that was relevant to her situation. Her writing might not be grammatical but it makes sense to me. You're looking at it with the eyes of a teacher.'

For a few minutes Sue was engrossed, shuffling and comparing pages. 'This parish priest – you don't think he's in on it as well?'

I didn't want to believe that. Lester was an outspoken opponent of a Government that had declared 'society' didn't exist while spending millions engineering it in the direction of those debatable Victorian values.

'It wasn't the impression I got. I don't think he'd have even mentioned Dulcie's claim to be in films if he'd known what sort.'

'Okay, so we can eliminate him. How many other men were in the photographs?'

'That's just it, apart from Cockburn whose size made him obvious, I don't know. I really only looked at one and I can't get *that* out of my head.'

I wanted to tell Sue that tonight she'd gone a long way to cauterising the image of Dulcie, but it would have meant telling her about Maureen or, at the very least, that I'd had a sexual encounter with somebody else. Besides, I couldn't rely on it never coming back and I didn't want to tempt fate by talking about it.

Instead I told her about my theory that Dulcie might have grabbed more photos than Mandy'd admitted to having. 'I know Mandy wasn't in any of the others that I saw, even at a glance, and it's improbable that she only appeared in one.'

'If she didn't destroy them where do you think she'd have hidden them?'

'The same place she hid the ones she gave me – up the chimney at her squat. And that, of course, means Catterell may have got them back. Mandy'd have told him that I took the photos, and where she kept the remaining ones if any. He'd have made her.'

Sue jumped up, dusting dog hairs off herself. 'I want to get in on the action – everybody else seems to be involved except me. I'm going to try and pin down Viv about this policeman.'

I started to say that that might not be a good idea, but she was already out the door and heading for the phone.

Ten minutes and many raised voices later she came back and flopped on the sofa. 'This bloke must carry a lot of clout to frighten her off like that. She says we're asking for trouble and she doesn't want to get involved.' Sue sat staring into the fire and I stayed quiet, letting her deal with the disappointment which I suspected was not just due to the discovery that there was corruption in the British Police Force.

After a while she said resentfully 'She didn't sound surprised when I used his name, as if she'd known all along – I mean, even before I showed her the photograph.'

I put an arm round her, but she was fidgety and after a minute, as if she'd had a divine inspiration, she said 'We could look for the missing photos!'

'But not tonight.'

'Why not?'

She said it with such passion that it made me smile.

'Why not?' she persisted. 'Give me one good reason.'

'Because,' I said, 'while you were on the phone I watched the weather forecast and, as usual, they got it wrong. Look out the window.'

It must have been snowing for some time before I'd noticed: real snow, not the half-hearted stuff we usually get on the coast, but big serious lumps hurtling out of the sky on a north-east wind. We pulled open the study curtains and watched it cutting diagonally through the lamplight.

'Let's go out in it,' said Sue. 'Come on, just round the churchyard and back. We can take Daisy.'

I couldn't refuse her twice in one evening.

We crunched through the layers on the pavement before turning in at the heavy wrought-iron gate, and stopped to admire the blizzard swirling round the yew trees and tomb-stones. The path had disappeared but we kept to where we thought it was, reluctant to spoil the white lawns. Daisy wasn't under the same compunction and snuffled about, puzzled by the lack of messages. We did two circuits of the church and returned home, happy at relinquishing the burden of being adult, if only for a little while.

When we went to bed we left the curtains open so that we could watch the blizzard. Sue was asleep in minutes and I lay awake, pleased with the blur of shadows on the ceiling and the silence that snow imposes. I resumed the list with Colette, Margaret Cavendish, Kate Chopin and Mary Elizabeth Coleridge, but didn't get further than Anne Dickson.

Retribution

Our part of the country had caught a freak storm, cutting us off for several miles south of London and from most of the counties bordering the west. I hoped Bill would ring me from Norfolk, but as the day wore on I got impatient and called the Probation Office to find out if they'd heard from him. The answerphone said nobody was available so I left a message and tuned into local radio. The reports were all of traffic chaos on the main roads with stranded cars, helicopter rescues, cancelled trains and power fail-ures. It stopped snowing at mid-day when the forecasters began predicting an overnight freeze. As if on cue all the lights went out and the central heating died. I foraged in the cupboard under the stairs for candles, got in a supply of logs and switched on the gas oven to heat up the freezing kitchen.

When the phone rang I snatched up the receiver, thinking it might be Bill, but it was Sue. She'd gone into work at 8.30 and had been out with Mrs Bennett most of the morning, attending a mare that somebody had tortured and abused before turning it loose in the night. Sue's voice had that hard edge that meant she was fighting to stay in control.

'We had to put it down in the end. I'll be back in about an hour. Did Bill ring?'

'Not yet.' I wanted to say more, to offer her something. There weren't any words to make it better.

By the time she got in I had hot soup ready, but she refused the food and sat next to the fire, shivering and withdrawn. She looked smaller, as if she was slowly imploding with emotion. I felt excluded and useless, but sat next to her holding one of her hands that lay cold and unresponsive in mine. When the phone rang again she patted my hand as if giving me permission to leave her. When I came back she hadn't moved, nor did she ask who had called. I sat with her a bit longer and then went into the kitchen. As I stood drinking the soup and watching birds pecking at the scraps I'd put out, I made up my mind to kill Catterell.

Bill was dead.

The phone call had been Viv asking to speak to Sue. I explained the situation and said I'd get Sue to ring back. 'No, it's for you really. Sue was so angry with me last night, it's the least I can do. I know you were pinning your hopes on him with that photograph – and maybe it would have worked. I don't know. I'm sorry . . . '

My first thought had been that somehow Catterell had engineered the accident. It wasn't the case, of course, but events were happening so fast they seemed to spill into one another. The one constant factor was Catterell. We'd never get him, not by legal means; nobody could fight his kind by going through the usual channels.

'Who was that on the phone?'

Sue had come into the kitchen and was standing beside me. I told her and for a while we watched silently as the starlings fought over a chunk of stale cake while a sparrow nipped in and out, snatching crumbs.

'He must have decided to come back early because he wanted to see me,' I said eventually. 'It happened last night not long after the snow started, apparently. The police say he skidded and went into the side of the new bridge they're building.'

The sparrow pounced on a hefty morsel and dodged a lethal yellow beak before flying off with its prize.

'That's that then.' Sue's voice sounded flat and lifeless.

'Yes, I suppose so.'

'I think I'll go home if you don't mind. I need some time to myself. If you want me tomorrow give me a ring.'

Momentarily, and unfairly, I felt irritated that she should be so devastated by the death of a horse, but I needed some space too, so I didn't argue.

When she'd gone I thought I should have persuaded her to stay, given her some of my time and attention. Instead I gave it to Catterell. He wasn't at the Sea Chalet when I rang and whoever answered the phone didn't know when he'd be back.

'This is his place of residence?'

'I don't know.' The voice wasn't evasive and I guessed it was probably one of the residents.

'But he does live here?'

'Oh yes. We all live here.'

'And is it nice – living there?' I thought I might as well ask.

'Oh yes.' She started to tell me how lovely it was and then broke off to speak to someone else – 'It's a lady, about Mr Catterell.'

'Who is it?'

This was John. Nobody else oozed such malice.

'It's Mig Hills, John – remember me?'

'What d'you want?'

'Well, I'd like my eyebrows back and the use of my collar bones. Apart from that . . . ' Retribution, revenge, justice. 'Where is he?'

'Not here.'

'You're a man of few words, John – nasty habits, but few words. Tell your owner to ring me.'

There wasn't any response from the other end, barring John's adenoidal breathing.

'Speak to me, John. Tell me you've understood.'

Was he one of Catterell's accumulations from the Community Care fiasco? I started to ask him if he would pass on the message, but he put the phone down.

The jug with the knives was still in the back of the kitchen cabinet where I'd stowed it a week ago. Was it only that recently? I got it out and emptied the contents onto the worktop. Among the blades was a brute of a Sabatier that made me shudder even when I used it on dead meat. I put it back and chose a small wooden-handled knife worn thin and wavy by long use; it fitted neatly into the sling.

When the power came back on I switched on the television and waited.

Catterell rang me in the middle of an inane show in which a nauseatingly artificial has-been singer was playing matchmaker to some embarrassingly naive 'guests'. It was so grim it was morbidly fascinating.

'Well Miss Hills, and what can I do for you?' He sounded like we were old friends rather than somebody he'd tried to barbecue.

'It's more what I can do for you.'

'Is there anything you can do for me *Miss H*? I doubt it.' He had a horrible oily chuckle. 'I very much doubt that. Still, it's nice to hear from you – after our little encounter the other night I thought you wouldn't want to keep in touch. But, there you are, I'm wrong again.'

I thought how nice it would be to slit his throat, if only to cut short that snickering laugh.

'You're often wrong, Catterell, and you have made one big mistake. Those weren't the only photographs Mandy had.' It was a long shot – he had only to check to negatives to see if I was telling the truth.

'Really? How interesting – and how good of you to tell me.'

Underneath the arrogance was a slight hesitance, so I kept quiet and let him stew.

'Why are you telling me this, Miss Hills?'

I'd got him! He couldn't figure it out. If there were extra photos why didn't I just hand them over to whoever I thought could make the best legal use of them? If there weren't, why was I provoking him? Hadn't the silly bitch got the message yet?

'I'm not doing it for you, Catterell. This is for me – after what you've put me through you owe me. If you want the pictures back you'll have to pay for them, just like you had to pay Mandy.'

'I've already told you, the money I gave to that slut wasn't for the photos –'

'Bullshit. Even if *you* weren't bothered about them, Cockburn would be – not to mention,' I added, savouring the moment, 'your bent policeman.'

I let that sink in before going on. 'Don't bother to come round looking for the snaps – they're not here, and I've got guests tonight. You'll meet me tomorrow and you'll bring, what shall we say? – £5,000. No, let's make it £10,000. A top-brass copper and a struck-off doctor must be worth £5,000 apiece.'

He didn't like it; tried to wriggle out, saying I was mad and the pictures weren't worth anything, so I knew I'd been right – some were missing.

He couldn't keep it up for long: 'Alright, just to keep you calm, I'll meet you –'

'Please yourself,' I said. 'You either bring the money or your snaps go to Scotland Yard. I'll ring you in the morning to tell you where we'll meet. Don't bring anybody with you – if you're not on your own the deal's off.'

I dropped the phone back, feeling pretty good. It was energising having Catterell at a disadvantage for once. Even if there weren't any more photographs he didn't want me on his back. He had to be there tomorrow.

My last call of the day was to Jack. He was having a great time since meeting a couple of the other Brusselites' sons who knew all the best places to go in the city, which I took to mean all the places their parents had forbidden them to go to. I listened to his voice, an obstruction in my throat preventing me from saying much, which was just as well – he'd have been embarrassed if I'd gushed on about how much I loved him.

148

I deliberately hadn't thought too deeply about the consequences for me of what I was about to do. Because if I did I'd never do it. But I had reasoned that Jack would be OK with Mark, that his father could offer him things I never could, get him out of this dump, give him a chance. Jack had outgrown me, I told myself, and Mark would do the right thing because he was Mark. He might even let Jack visit me if . . .

After I'd put the phone down I sat on the loo and grizzled into the toilet roll, trying to wash out the emotion that logic couldn't quite overcome.

Then I wrote a letter to Sue, instructing her to call Mark if anything happened to me (I didn't specify what). I didn't try to explain what I was about to do because I didn't know whether I could, even suspected it would all end in farce. But it would end somehow.

Revenge

The taxi firm bumped me up a fiver because of the weather, even though the main roads were negotiable. Gritters and salters had cleared the bus routes, but the side roads were treacherous. When we got to the street with the squat he refused to drive down it. 'Look at the bloody drifts – I'm not risking my cab down there.'

I paid him and got out. Even in the snow the terrace looked bleak with its gaping basement areas and hard grey bricks. The cab backed, its plume of exhaust blue-grey against the clinical whiteness; it left tyre tracks and a dying trail of music on the still air. Gingerly I crossed the road and hugged the cold railings down the sloping pavement, hanging on with my good arm. I nearly came a cropper on the steps down to the squat, lurching against the loose inside railings, which hurt like hell. Before I went further I peered over the snow drift on the pavement to make sure nobody was around, and then continued on down to the basement door and into the dense and smelly blackness of the hallway.

The laser-slim torch beam slid along the passage to a lino-covered flight of stairs leading up into the dark of the house. I climbed a few steps, poking the light ahead of me onto a landing leading to a couple of doors and the next staircase. Apart from the grit beneath my feet and the moaning of wind in the chimneys the building held its breath. I returned to the basement and entered Mandy's room. Either Catterell or vandals had wrecked what domesticity she'd imposed on it. The tarpaulin had been torn from the window, her gas lamp lay on the floor, its globe smashed, and her make-up was scattered among lumps of broken brick and the spilt contents of her food store. The violent red of a lipstick caught my eye and I picked it up, remembering the clown-coloured mouth in the deadwhite face.

There wasn't anything hidden in the chimney; I stretched as far as I could, grunting against the pressure on my collar bones, my fingers dislodging clumps of sticky soot that tumbled down my arm into the grate. Mandy was smaller than me – her arms couldn't have stretched further than mine. I made a perfunctory search of the two base-ment rooms and then went out to look for a telephone box. Opposite the terrace was the high wall of an aban-doned brewery that stretched the whole length of the street. I followed it down to the next road which led even-tually into a pedestrianised shopping centre. A couple of shops were open but nobody was buying and the women assistants stood around looking bored out of their minds.

The first phone was smarmed with what looked like ice cream but could have been shaving foam, so I tried the next. That didn't work so I went back to the other one and punched in Catterell's number, holding the sticky receiver away from my ear.

Catterell answered, trying to sound casual, but I cut him short before he got into his patronising stride: 'Have you got the money?'

'Of course,' he lied.

'You've got five minutes to get to Mandy's squat. I'll be watching from the top floor – it gives a good view of the surrounding streets so don't bring your rottweiler with you.'

'How do I know you haven't got anyone with *you*?' he asked.

'You don't, but unlike you I'm not a liar,' I lied. 'There's no need for anyone else: you'll hand over the money, I'll give you the photos and we go our separate ways.'

It took me four minutes to get back to the house and onto the second landing. There wasn't any need to go to the top – from the second floor I could see both ends of the street and, through the disintegrating brewery wall, the road I'd just come out of. Taking care to avoid the jagged fins of glass still clinging to the broken window frame, I leant forward and waited.

The room was bitterly cold. Snow had blown in and was piled up in sharp ridges between the door and the window. My finger tips were numb as I eased the knife out of my pocket and slid it into the sling. Catterell was eight minutes late. He parked the Mercedes at the top of the street where the taxi had dropped me off, and I kept my eyes on it as he slithered along the pavement. I was expecting to see John pop up from the back seat but there was no sign of him. Catterell was stumbling on the rubble in the passageway and calling my name. I took one last look up and down the street and went down to meet him.

He was waiting at the bottom of the stairs. I put my right hand inside the sling and gripped the knife, and as I went down I was calculating that at about two risers above him a downward plunge into the neck anywhere inside the open collar of his ludicrous fur coat would inflict a deep and hopefully lethal wound. My hand was tingling where it held the narrow wooden handle, as if the knife itself vibrated with energy. I could see in my mind the thin warped blade puncturing first a hole and then a slit as it sunk, slicing through veins and muscle to get at the shuddering heart or the spongy fibre of a lung; and then the hot blood, sliding up the knife like a well gushing red oil.

As I reached the critical spot Catterell turned and went into the basement.

By the time I got inside the room he was facing me, a superior smile on his lips. He was a good six inches taller than me and the coat made him look bigger than he was, which was probably half the point of wearing it. There wasn't much chance of getting in a sufficiently-disabling blow while he was standing.

'I haven't got much time – where are the pictures?'

'Where's the money?'

He laughed: 'I don't buy before I've seen the merchandise.'

I indicated the chimney: 'She hid them up there – I'm surprised you didn't torture that out of Mandy before you murdered her.'

There was an odd look in his eyes that might have been apprehension or excitement. 'Yes, so am I,' he said. He kept his eyes on me as he moved towards the fireplace, then bent down and cast a quick glance up the flue. I moved a couple of steps forward, my feet kicking a piece of brick, and he stood up quickly. 'I've got a better idea – you get them down for me.'

'Afraid to get your hands dirty?'

'Very amusing, Miss Hills. No, I don't fancy turning my back on a woman. You're such devious creatures.'

It was my turn to laugh. 'You're such a dickhead, Catterell. You can't be seriously frightened by a mere woman – a disabled one at that.'

He wouldn't be provoked, but went and stood by the window, waving a hand to clear my way to the fireplace. I was just as watchful as him while I crouched in the hearth, making a big show of discomfort as I pretended to search for the pictures.

'I can't do it,' I said at last. 'I can't get my arm up high enough.'

He sighed. 'Alright – but step back. That'll do.'

I was no more than four feet away from him when a movement outside on the area steps drew my attention away from him. I saw, in what seemed the same moment, a leg in flared trousers, then Catterell standing up too quickly. I slashed out with the knife. It missed Catterell by miles, but his foot slipped off the hearth and he half-fell into the alcove beside the fireplace. As I ran up the stairs John appeared in the outer doorway. I reached the first landing and was halfway along it when a hand shot through the stair-rail and grabbed my ankle. Catterell glared at me from the stairwell. I tried to shake free from his grip and when he wouldn't let go, twisted round and stamped on his wrist.

The first door in front of me wouldn't open and in panic I climbed to the next landing. In the snow-filled bedroom I hurled myself against the door, slamming it shut, and yelping with pain. All I could think of was Catterell's excitement, the face animated first by the fun of it all, and then with shock as my heel battered his hand.

Just before he launched himself at the door I heard him yelling 'Get up here, you stupid bastard.'

Then he was in the room. I jumped back to avoid being hit by the door, jabbing at him with the knife, but he hardly seemed to notice, ploughing straight into me and slamming me against the wall, his weight turning the knife uselessly sideways between us.

Loose ends

I must have pushed him really hard. I don't remember. One minute his arms were flailing like windmill sails as his feet slipped on the snow, and then he was going backwards over the low window sill. He stuck his arms out to save himself, his fingers clawing long strips off the wallpaper, grabbing at the rotting window frame, and finally, frantically, even at the bits of remaining glass on which they left bright red smears.

John, panting with the effort of his sprint up the stairs, crossed the room and looked out of the window. I braced myself, trying to get a proper grip on the knife which was vibrating as I held it. I was thinking of making a run for it when he said 'Oh!'

He said it like a child would on discovering something a bit naughty. I couldn't see his face because the nylon-fringed snorkel on his anorak was still up, but his hands were clasping and unclasping with a kind of helpless agitation as he stared down into the basement. He turned to look at me accusingly: 'Look what you done.'

I eased myself off the wall. 'Get out of the way. Move.'

He looked uncertain. 'You'll catch it now.'

I flicked the knife sideways and he stepped away from the window.

Catterell was hanging by his neck from the inside railings. The weight of his body had wedged him between two of the ornate finials that topped the iron stakes. His eyes stared up at me.

John was shuffling about and muttering anxiously. He followed me down the stairs, telling me off as if I'd broken a window pane instead of his boss's neck. 'You'n'alf in trouble,' he kept saying.

He was still saying it as I stood in front of Catterell's corpse. The neck had turned the colour of a rotten orange where the muscles had been torn by the drop. One Gucci dangled about six inches from the ground; the other shoe was upside-down near the doorway. Although I knew he was dead, I couldn't convince myself that he wouldn't suddenly look down at me and with that snickering laugh say something – like 'I've got you now.'

'What we going to do?' John moaned, wringing his hands as if it was his fault.

I shared some of his anguish, but not much. Sudden, violent death was frightening, but for Catterell it had been too sudden. And even though death was what I'd had in mind for him, imagining it was not the same as seeing it, particularly this close. All the weeks of learning to hate and fear him had ended so abruptly I couldn't come to terms with him dangling there, helplessly.

What *were* we – was I – going to do? Catterell had become his own evidence: the one remaining photograph, what was left of it, could still be 'lost', but the police couldn't very well lose a body. Pope might be powerful, but even he couldn't magic away a corpse. Could he?

There was one loose end dangling in my mind and that was the tape that Mandy had mentioned, the one containing evidence of Pope and Cockburn's involvement, filmed at the same time as the photographs were taken. That would be too-easily destroyed, unless I got to it first.

I became aware that I was stamping my feet to bring some warmth back into them, and that John was doing the same, although he wouldn't come any nearer than the foot of the steps. He looked more embarrassed and fretful than frightened. We could have been waiting for a bus, except for the hanging body from which the smell of sud-denly-emptied bowel and bladder was beginning to make its presence felt in the cold air.

'Get the car keys,' I told John.

He looked at me in horror: 'Mr Catterell don't like nobody messing about with his Merc.'

Gingerly I went through the pockets of the dead animal Catterell was wearing and then reluctantly foraged in his trousers pockets until I found the keys.

'Can you drive?'

John shook his head inside the snorkel but allowed himself to be ushered up the steps. From the other side of the street the body was not visible, the head hidden behind a snowdrift. I got John back to the car and belted him in to the front passenger seat. He was still rabbiting on, more to himself than me, when I started the engine, silently thanking Catterell for owning a left-hand drive automatic. I one-handed the car a couple of blocks away from the squat and then stopped.

'Okay John, take off your hood and concentrate – and for Christ's sake shut up. Who's at the Sea Chalet this morning?'

'I dunno.'

'Yes you do. Who's there apart from the usual resi-dents? Is Dr Cockburn there?' He shook his head sulkily. 'Somebody in charge – a matron?'

'Mrs Dunwoody!' He said it as if he'd got a question right in a quiz. 'But she's not there all Sunday – she goes to . . . somewhere else.'

'Who looks after the residents on Sundays?'

John 'erred' a bit and chewed the corner of his anorak. 'Mike does the dinner, in the kitchen.'

'And who serves the dinner?'

'We do, me and the others. We shouldn't be in Mr Catterell's car – he don't like –'

'I know,' I said. 'But today it's okay because he's dead and there's not a damn thing he can do about it.'

That started John off again about the hot water I was in, and he was going to tell because it wasn't nothing to do with him.

'Who you going to tell?' I asked. 'You do as I tell you now. Right? Right.'

I rolled myself a cigarette and offered him one. 'Gives you cancer,' he said, piously, but he seemed pleased that I'd offered.

I started up the car and eased us along the roads towards the hostel area. An off-licence was open and I stopped to buy some Anadin to quell the fire that was screeching up my neck and down the left shoulder.

'Want anything?' I asked as I got out. 'Observer?'

That was mean, so I offered him an ice cream. 'Can I come too?' he said; by the tone of his voice he seemed to expect me to say no.

It was like a major expedition. He took ages deciding what flavour he wanted and I had to keep reminding myself that this was the monster who poured bleach down women's throats when he wasn't helping to set fire to them.

When we got back in the car he seemed to have forgotten about his employer hanging from the railings and to have accepted me as the natural successor. I washed down the tablets with some tonic water and watched him making a mess of himself with the chocolate-chip cone.

'Good, eh?'

He grunted with pleasure. Catterell was twice as big a shit as I'd thought he was.

'I'll tell you what we're going to do, John. You listening? Good. You're going to show me over your hotel and if anybody asks we're going to say Mr Catterell said it was alright because I'm going to work there.'

How long would it be before someone discovered the body? – it was a back street and it was cold. Until the snow melted or the smell attracted some passer-by or somebody's dog came home with an unusual bone? It could be days. But he'd be missed before then.

'What I specially want to see – here, use a tissue – is

Mr Catterell's apartment, or his office. He has got one?'

'I mustn't go in there,' John slurped.

'But if I say you can, is that okay?'

The little eyes of indeterminate colour regarded me suspiciously. 'Mr Catterell doesn't like you. He says you're an interfering bitch.'

'But he's dead, John. Gone, for good. He can't give you any more orders or tell you what to do, or call you a stupid bastard, ever again. That's okay, isn't it?'

'I gotta have a pee.'

'As soon as we get to the Sea Chalet. Look at me – no, properly. I'm in charge now. You have to do what I say. You can forget Catterell – I've got his keys – look.'

I held up the bunch I'd taken from Catterell's pocket as if they represented my authority. 'So I'm the boss now.'

'You're the boss,' said John.

'That's right. And don't tell anybody what's happened to him, either.'

I started up the engine, then switched it off. 'You know those photos that Catterell was after? Were you in any of them?' I couldn't recall seeing him in any of them, but that didn't mean he wasn't there.

He was anxious to find the right answer, but all he came up with was 'I dunno.'

'Did you help him take pictures of Dulcie and Mandy?'

John shook his head emphatically, as if he wouldn't do such a thing. And I believed him. I put his mental age at about eight, he was that transparent in his reactions.

'You killed Dulcie, didn't you,' I said gently. 'Did you know what you were doing it for?'

'Didn't,' he said, wriggling in the seat, either because of his bladder or his embarrassment.

'Didn't what?'

'Didn't kill her.'

'Who poured bleach down her throat, then?'

'I didn't know what it was,' he said, close to tears now. 'Mr Catterell said "Grab her" in the alley and she was screaming like, on the ground, and he said she needed a drink. And he had this bottle . . . '

'Then what happened?'

'He made her say what she done with the photos and

157

then he said to put the bottle in her mouth. And then she started screaming and then she stopped, but she wasn't dead. She was -'

'Never mind,' I said quickly. 'Tell me about Dr Cockburn – did he come to the hostel often?'

I waited while John's mis-matched cogs tried to mesh.

'He did come sometimes,' he said thoughtfully, pleased, I think, that the spotlight was off him.

'What did he do while he was there?'

'Went upstairs with Mr Catterell.'

'To do what?'

'I don't know. I wasn't allowed up there.'

'Did other men arrive with Dr Cockburn?'

John grabbed his crutch: 'I gotta go to the toilet.'

Video niceies

There was a public lavatory on the clifftop, so I drove him there, saw him in the door and waited outside in case he tried to do a runner. Men going in and out looked at me curiously, wondering why I was waiting so close to the doorway. It wasn't until we were back in the car that I noticed he'd forgotten to zip up his flares.

'You were telling me who went to the Sea Chalet with Dr Cockburn,' I reminded him.

'Oh yeah . . . I don't know their names. I just answered the door and showed them up. They used to tip me.'

'Was there a Mr Pope? No? Okay – one last question – do your zip up – how did Mandy die?'

John did a bit more squirming and close analysis of his hands. 'You hurt me,' he said barely audibly. 'You sprayed that stuff in my eye.'

Patience, Hills. 'I'm sorry. Now about Mandy –'

'It stung.'

'Not as much as being set fire to.'

John lapsed into a sulky silence. There was a can of WD40 on the parcel shelf. I picked it up and took the top off: 'About Mandy . . . '

'You could make somebody blind, doing that,' John whined.

I jammed the top back on and chucked the can on the back seat. 'Alright, I'm not going to use it. Just tell me who killed her.'

After he'd told me I drove on to the Sea Chalet. It was lunchtime and the place smelt of roast meat and greens, plates of which were being carried with studied care and concentration from somewhere below stairs to a dining room opposite the TV lounge. A little man with ferocious eyes and a sunken mouth stopped in mid-shuffle and told John that 'Mike' was looking for him.

'You're supposed to help on Sundays,' he said, bossily. The tray he was holding was at an angle and gelatinous gravy was slithering off the plates. John looked at me helplessly.

I put a hand out and lifted the tray at the corner. 'John's got the day off – Mr Catterell's orders. You're losing your gravy again.'

The little man got in a tizz and I pushed John towards the stairs. We passed the room where I was supposed to have met Sidney Prince, and climbed to the top floor. A door marked 'Private' was locked and I went through the keys from Catterell's pocket until I found a Yale that fitted. John wouldn't cross the threshold because he'd 'get into trouble' so I made him promise to stay at the top of the stairs and let me know if anyone came up.

I don't know what I expected – ceiling mirrors and brothel-black sheets probably; anyway, the first room was just an office with filing cabinets, a safe and a computer. Beyond was a large lounge with a plastic chandelier, genuine green Chesterfield, and a cocktail bar fronted by spindly high stools. The latest flat-screen telly stood in one corner under a shelf for a video and about a hundred tapes. I groaned. If I had to go through that lot I'd be here all day. Either Catterell has amazingly eclectic taste or he entertained children up there, which was a nasty thought. Pavarotti, Rambo, Fantasia, Police Academies 1–100, The Railway Children – no Miss Whiplash or Deep Throat.

My mother could have slept in his bedroom without

any qualms, excepting maybe for the anatomically-gross female nude (what other kind is there?) in a cheap frame that hung over the pink draylon headboard. The drawers contained what drawers should and the MFI wardrobe was a disappointment of Catterell-style suits and shoes.

I examined a few of the videos to see if the covers concealed more imflammatory titles, but they seemed genuine. What would a creep like Catterell get out of light comedy and children's films? Fast-forwarding a couple on the video produced nothing more incriminating than juvenile taste.

John was still outside the office door, looking guilty and uncomfortable.

'What you doing?' he implored. 'Somebody'll come. We'll get found out.'

'Those tapes in there – is there a video downstairs for the residents?'

John looked even more agitated: 'You mustn't touch them – that's the video library. We have to borrow them and then they have to go back to Mr Catterell. Can we go now?'

'In a minute.'

Back in the lounge I got a chair and stood on it to reach the tapes on the top shelf. What would be the most likely title to disguise the ones I was looking for? The Goonies – Bambi – Wizard of Oz? I ran the tapes through the video far enough to see that they were what they claimed to be, and gave up. Even men like Catterell had patches of ordinary living in their otherwise grubby lives. As I re-entered the office I could hear voices drifting up the stairs and guessed that lunch was over. I didn't expect any of the residents to come up here, but I wasn't confident that John would remain at his post to warn me if they did, and sure enough when I stuck my head round the door the landing was deserted. I got far enough down the stairs to see people returning to or coming out of their rooms, but no John. The fierce-looking man was just below me, telling everybody else what to do and generally making a nuisance of himself.

'You have to wear your coats and gloves before you go out. Be at the front door in two ticks.' He stuck his head in one of the rooms: 'Come on Julia, it's time to go, you'll make us late.'

Julia didn't sound like she wanted to go so Rumplestiltskin said 'Mrs Dunwoody' would be ever so peeved if Julia made them miss the start of the concert. 'Fuck Mrs Dunwoody,' said Julia, which sent the little man hopping downstairs like a malignant frog to tell on her.

I sneaked back to the office and locked the door behind me. I didn't fancy tackling somebody with a formidable name like Dunwoody and just hoped John wasn't blabbing downstairs. He might have just scarpered in which case I'd wait until the happy band had left for their concert and then make my exit too. In the meantime . . .

None of the keys fitted the safe, so I switched on the computer, took off my coat and settled down to go through the directory. There were about a dozen documents, most of them to do with finances and referring to two other hostels besides the Sea Chalet. There were lists of residents in all three, but neither Dulcie nor Mandy appeared, although Sidney was still there with the date of November 3rd terminating his residency. He'd been at the Sea Chalet for eight years and in the column headed 'Next of Kin' was 'Nil', which must have been very convenient. I doubted whether Catterell would keep anything really important on the hard disc – and since I was nearly innumerate I didn't know whether there was anything significant about his bookkeeping. But Sue could find her way through any maze of figures; she had the sort of mind that retained the complexities of animal anatomy and Mozart scores but would read the ends of novels first because she couldn't be bothered to wade through the narrative. If Catterell kept floppy discs I could copy his documents and she could analyse them for me.

The locks on his desk yielded to the same key and in his bottom drawer were three floppies. Two contained documents but the third was blank. I must have been in the apartment for an hour when I began transferring the contents of the hard disc.

I didn't hear anybody come in. Not then. Later the whisper of draught-excluder brushing carpet bubbled up out of the memory banks.

The computer was noisily absorbing the last document and I was leaning back in the chair when this wasp stung me, just below and behind the right ear. That's what I thought it was, a wasp. I clapped my hand to my neck, inhaling sharply at the pain, and started to stand up. My lungs flooded with a pungent odour like expensive disinfectant: I didn't plunge into the black vortex of literary tradition, nor did my vision go wavy or the sound echoey like it does in the films. I just went.

The female sex

When I came back it was to a nice, cosy, relaxed warm world with nice Dr Cockburn waiting for me.

'There you are, John,' he was saying. 'I told you she wasn't dead.' He smiled beatifically at me; he had a lovely bedside manner. 'Not yet.'

That did concern me, intellectually, but there wasn't any emotional back-up. He could have threatened to saw my legs off and I'd have been interested but not involved. Whatever illegal substance he'd doped me with was wonderful stuff. The ability to rationalise was intact but banished to the backwoods of my mind, leaving my body out front to enjoy its euphoria.

Cockburn was a slug: huge, fat-fingered, hairless, but a lovely dresser. Men can get away with being fat. Their clothes are tailored to conceal not reveal, and his suit was a masterpiece of pin-striped, sartorian cunning, contributing to his air of authority that was at odds with his face. That was the guileless face of a boy, although he must have been past 60. His eyes were pale blue above an unfinished blob of a nose, and his full lips were set in baby-fat cheeks. Put a white beard on him and you'd got everybody's idea of Father Christmas, except that when you looked closely the eyes were brightly cold.

He smoothed my forehead with a spongy hand and looked at me with something akin to pride as if I was a fascinating disease he'd finally discovered after years of research.

'You've led us quite a dance, Mig.' The ennunciation was beautiful, the voice perfectly controlled. 'What an odd name. Is it supposed to indicate how lethal you can be, like the aircraft?'

While he mocked me my exiled brain was trying to make a comeback and I was going to tell him something unpleasant, but the thought got a poor reception from my vocal chords.

Cockburn smiled indulgently. 'Don't try to speak, you can't. You can't move at all – the wonders of modern medicine. Let me show you.'

He jabbed a porky finger into my left shoulder and beamed. 'See? Not real pain, is it?'

Not to him, maybe, but to me it was like a deep chord vibrating through the broken bone. It summoned my brain closer to appreciate its depth and intensity, and silently I voiced its enormity until it died away.

'It is terrible when one cannot express pain in physical movement,' said Cockburn, peering at me intently. 'Not even to shut one's eyes, which express so much, particularly a woman's eyes. I really do believe they are the proverbial window of her soul – if she actually has one. That is debatable, Mig – what was that ditty of Samuel Butler's? "The souls of women are so small/That some believe they've none at all". Seventeenth century nonsense, of course, but did you know' – he jabbed me again, as if to increase my concentration – 'that as late as 1940 – are you listening, Mig? – as late as 1940 The Catholic Encyclopedia printed something to the effect that "the female sex is in some respects" . . . how does it go? . . . "inferior to the male sex in body and soul". And do you know,' he said, jabbing me again, 'I really do believe they've got something there.'

My brain had reasserted itself enough to activate my voice, but it was merely a low growling that could have meant anything, even pleasure.

'And so masochistic! One of my heroes, the late and incontestably great, Somerset Maugham, pointed out that a woman will always sacrifice herself if given the opportunity because it's her favourite form of self-indulgence.'

Cockburn leant so close that my long-sight blurred his features. 'I can indulge you, Mig,' he breathed as if I was on the end of an obscene phone call, 'to an extent you had not realised possible. I could make your dreams of masochism reach the ultimate.'

While Cockburn indulged himself describing what heights he could take my mythological masochism to, I was having my own problems. Saliva was building up in the back of my throat and I had a horrible premonition that I wasn't going to be able to swallow and would drown in my own spit. The windows of my debatable soul must have been semaphoring distress signals because he stopped in mid-fantasy, hoiked me upright on the Chesterfield and began massaging my neck.

'Better? Good. Can't lose my patient. Now where was I? Never mind – the deed done is better than the word uttered. And I promise you, it will be done.' He beamed, and then laughed. 'Aren't I a villain.' I swear if he'd had moustaches he'd have twirled them, he was that far gone. 'You're a bit of a villain yourself, Mig – what *did* you do to James? John's been telling me about your escapade this morning, but he's not very articulate and I would rather hear it from you.'

I wondered whether the twinkle ever left his eyes – and what happened when it did – and if it was still there now. Since he'd sat me up I'd been staring fixedly at the shelves of video tapes and couldn't see his face.

When he bent forward to peer at me he was still beaming away: 'Of course, you can't tell me, can you! But you will. The effects of my little concoction are wearing off even now – I couldn't make it too potent or you wouldn't have been able to breathe.

'Are those genuine tears? Or just the usual disgusting female secretions?' He flourished an immaculate white handkerchief and delicately wiped my cheeks. 'It must be uncomfortable not being able to close one's eyelids. What are you staring at so intently? Ah, the tapes! Of course. That's what you came for. But Mig, even an incompetent pimp like James wouldn't keep materials like that in such an accessible place. I'd have made sure of that.'

Cockburn jingled the keys I'd taken from Catterell's body in front of my face. 'Quite useless. Not only do they not include the key to the safe, which is the first place any unimaginative person would look, but they aren't even necessary, because the tapes are not locked away.'

This time when he came closer I could smell him: the not entirely-unpleasant hint of fresh sweat mixed with a citrus perfume. 'You're not an unimaginative woman, Mig, are you?' He wagged a finger at me. 'James had you wrong. He took you for just another interfering, frigid woman who wanted to spoil the boys' fun.'

The finger stopped wagging and hooked itself into the neck of my jumper, pulling it down. 'Let's see what we have here,' he murmured. 'Ah, yes, I see them – the woman's symbol and the double-headed axe signifying female strength. Is that what it's all about, Mig! You're the female warrior avenging oppressed womanhood?.'

Cockburn laughed and patted my cheek. 'Sweet. But misguided. Men always have and always will oppress women, that's the natural way, and you are swimming against a biological tide. The majority of women never will rebel against a destiny dictated by hormones and when one does, to paraphrase Nietzsche, "There is usually something wrong with her sex organs"'

Cockburn leant back in his chair. 'Look at me. I know you can.'

I swivelled my eyes, meaning to put as much contempt into them as I felt.

'Good girl. Now Cinders, you shall go to the ball. For your tenacity and lovable muddle-headedness, you shall see the tapes.'

Cockburn stood up and moved towards the bedroom door. 'No doubt you looked in here? Didn't you think it odd that a man should have a pink headboard above his bed? It's a cheap feminine touch in an otherwise masculine bedroom, a left-over from the bad old days when James had a wife. He would have got rid of it with as much conscience as he got rid of her, except that it serves a purpose, which is – you've guessed! To hide behind its obscene pink bulges . . . '

He almost twirled into the bedroom out of sight. I

swivelled my eyes enough to pick up John standing in the doorway to the office, like a dog waiting for its master. It took more than an ice cream to buy his loyalty. I tried to say 'Help me' but it came out as "ellee' and he looked away, embarrassed.

Cockburn came back bearing two tapes as if they were the Holy Grail. 'These are the mastertapes of our latest enterprise. While I'm deciding what to do with you we'll have a film show. These, my dear deviant, are so much better than mere photographs, particularly the second one, copies of which will wing their way round the world bringing endless pleasure to men of rare taste.'

And lots of dosh for Cockburn.

'This one,' he said, sliding it into the machine, is not so professional, except that it includes one or two participants who, at the right time, will pay either in deed or hard cash for their pleasures.'

He sat beside me and pressed the remote control. 'John, you can wait in the office. Shut the door behind you.'

Having the stills in my head was bad enough. The shit unfolding before me would stick for ever. I willed my eyelids to function or my head to turn and was rewarded with one shut eye and a slight inclining of my neck. The view of Cockburn stroking his thighs wasn't much of an alternative but, provided he didn't start stroking mine, I could put up with it. Not for long, though.

Despite the fact that there was sound on the tape he kept up a running commentary on the merits of the performers, including himself.

'Mig, you not watching! I'm no Michael Winner but I thought my direction had great cinematic potential. And my choice of cast was inspired – there's a market for these mental hospital scenarios. It's a pity this one won't be on general release. You don't realise how privileged you are,' he said, lifting my chin until the screen was in full view again. 'Do feel free to comment – when you're able.'

I managed 'oring crap' and he chuckled. 'Perhaps you're right – not for the afficionado, too tame. Now this next one . . .' He got up and changed the tapes. 'Up until now the Americans have cornered the market and I must admit this one is more the result of opportunism than a carefully-planned production. However, it has the advantage of being spontaneous which some of the current output lacks.'

The twinkle disappeared for a moment.

'Nictate by all means – it keeps the eyeballs clean – but if you shut them deliberately I will remove them.'

I didn't doubt him. Catterell had been a nasty bit of work, but he was a Mickey Mouse compared to Cockburn. It wasn't just because Catterell was no longer a threat: my fear of him had been mingled with contempt for the posturing of a shabby, jumped-up oik. He was vulgar and somehow that made him destructible, just like me. Now here was this justifiably-confident, authoritarian male who could quote Nietzche, knew the significance of the double-headed axe, and had probed my motivation with humiliating accuracy. I didn't just fear his ability to carry out his threat – I feared *him*, his easy confidence, his knowldge, his smell, his automatic right to power that maleness gave him and which he knew how to use.

John's account of Mandy's murder hadn't prepared me for the actuality of it. His own involvement in her abuse before she died explained his dogged 'loyality' to Cockburn, who probably threatened him with exposure like he would one day threaten Pope and the other men in the first film.

He'd cast John in the role of well-hung plebian idiot through whose gross bestiality 'men of rare taste' could work off their own misogyny wiile retaining a sense of superiority over him. Cockburn didn't appear, except as a pair of fat hands in rubber gloves administering the lethal dose of heroin to a terrified Mandy to whom he carefully explained, while she was trussed and gagged, exactly what was going to happen to her.

The nightmare rolled on for 20 minutes – I counted them on the video clock while surreptitiously flexing muscles and trying to work out what Cockburn had planned for me.

When the screen went blank he stayed in his chair and both of us waited for him to give utterance to his thoughts. He got as far as 'Hmmm' and then lapsed into silence.

My neck and shoulders were beginning to ache, signal-
ling the return of feeling. Just beside me on a nest of
DIY-store tables was an unlit lamp, one of those glass
bottles of water containing blobs of oil that floated sick-
eningly about when the temperature rose, and which
were much sought-after kitzch these days. I had it in
mind to smash Cockburn on the head with it, but when I
tentatively raised my arm it felt like lead.

'An improvement on the first,' Cockburn was saying.
'Lacking in raw violence, but one or two subtle touches.
What do you think?'

'I think,' I said with difficulty, 'that your sister would
have you put away if she knew.'

We're all vulnerable somewhere, and I was trying to
find Cockburn's underbelly.

'My sister,' he said, thoughtfully. 'What are you playing
at, Mig? Trying to conjure up a sisterhood that doesn't
exist? Calling on the monstrous regiment to save you? My
sister –' he stood up and leaned over me; he was mad,
but he wasn't angry '– is a self-centred, whinging little
snob who's never forgiven me for being cleverer than
her. Did you try to recruit her? You poor deluded – I'm
more sympathetic to your cause than she is! Ah, Mig, you
disappoint me. You think because she's a woman she'd
understand you? She loathes your kind. She wants power,
just the same as you do, but she'd climb on the back of
any other woman to get it. I've seen her do it.'

He looked at me sadly. 'You're so predictable after all,'
he said, as if he had been hunting a tiger and found a
rabbit. Then, used to a life of disappointingly miniscule
people, he abruptly reverted to his twinkling self, glanced
at his watch and said 'Mrs Dunwoody will be back soon
with her flock. It's time we made a move. I had thought
of giving you the star role in my next production – one
with more guts, but we'd need a soundproof room. Never
mind. You can make your debut in your own private picture show.'

He left me to think about that while he used the word
processor in the office to write my 'epitaph', which I took
to mean a suicide note.

I rolled off the couch and crab-walked over to the
video on top of which was the Dulcie tape, which I

stuffed into the sling between my arm and ribs, then replaced it with 'The Sound of Music' after peeling off the handwritten label. Cockburn was still punching the word processor as I crawled across the carpet to the oil-blob lamp beside which was a cordless telephone. I dialled Sue's number, willing her to answer, my eyes fixed on the office doorway. The chatter of a daisy-wheel meant Cockburn had nearly finished. Come on, come on -

'Hallo.'

I got as far as 'I'm at the Sea Chalet' when Cockburn appeared in the doorway, brandishing a sheet of A4. His fingers hooked onto my wrist and tore the phone out of my hand; and then he stood listening to Sue's frantic voice, his head cocked, his fat lips parted in a half-smile, before he cut her off. I cringed, expecting some sort of retribution, but he merely hauled me up like a rag doll and dumped me back on the Chesterfield. I thought he'd ask me who I'd called and was seriously considering a tour de force of hysterics to gain time while Sue called the police, but when I drew in a preparatory breath I realised there wasn't enough energy left for anything so diverting. Instead I said 'That was the police.'

Cockburn slow-hand clapped my effort. 'I don't think so – you haven't had much luck in that direction. Another of your axe-wielding women is probably nearer the truth – I see it is. That could present interesting possibilities: two or even three of you for the price of one.'

He bent down and thrust his face within inches of mine. There wasn't the faintest glimmer of a twinkle in the pale blue. 'Pity I haven't got the time. Sign this.'

He dropped the A4 and a ballpoint into my lap. It was a corny creation of the goodbye-cruel-world variety, but I'd been to enough inquests to know that the verdict would be 'suicide while the balance of the mind was disturbed', which would slot in neatly with a received wisdom that women are generally emotionally unstable anyway. I wondered how I could sign it so that somebody would be able to say 'She never signed her name that way', but it wouldn't matter – some suicides don't sign their last messages, while others sign off in ways that only reinforce the verdict. What Cockburn didn't know was that, in a way, I'd already written a fond farewell which was lying on my dining table and addressed to Sue. A coroner might think it odd that I'd left two notes.

Cockburn sent John downstairs to make sure nobody was about and, without inspecting either of them, put the two tapes in his briefcase. When John returned the two of them half-carried me downstairs, stopped at a peg-rack to take a long woolly scarf which was wound tightly round my nose and mouth, and propelled me out the back door into the hostel's small, high-walled backyard and Cockburn's Audi. Even if we were seen people would think it was just another wobbly being carted off, and good riddance, too.

John was delegated to keep me quiet in the back seat, which he did by sitting as close to me as he could without actually getting on my lap, one hand poised around my shoulder to give it a hug, as per his master's instructions, and the other within reach of my mouth to stifle any screams that would inevitably result. He needn't have bothered: I was out of ideas and had lapsed into a state of passivity due more to fear than the effects of the drug. That had almost worn off, but I was so scared by now that physical action seemed an impossibility. I kept thinking about what Cockburn meant when he said I'd have my own private picture show.

Second thoughts

The adrenalin started to flow when the hostel's Dormobile turned in at the open gates as we were driving out. I thought if I could get my face close enough to the Audi's tinted windows maybe Mrs Dunwoody, or whoever was driving the van, would see me.

The two vehicles were within inches of one another but before I could make a move Cockburn said quietly 'Try anything and John will reset that collar bone.'

Then we were out of the gates and going down the street.

There weren't many people about and not a lot of traffic. What we did encounter swept obliviously on. Cockburn drove west across town, past a park where children and parents were sledging and snowballing; past the garish lights of a fast-food restaurant where families were feeding; past a police car sorting out an accident on a slippery side road. The normality of it all further entrenched me in the abnormality of my own situation.

Before John could stop me I pulled the scarf off my mouth and asked where we were going.

'To fantasy land,' said Cockburn, regarding me briefly in the driving mirror.

I still didn't understand what he meant when he turned onto the coastal road leading to the bird reserve.

'Isn't this where you live out your fantasies, Mig?' he said, indicating the bay with its iron-grey mud flats stark against the fields of snow. 'What do you dream about when you're tramping about in this wilderness? Putting the world to rights? Matriarchal domination? Or is it the more common female fantasy of romance and rape? No, you'd resist that, wouldn't you.'

Dusk was gathering as he pulled in behind the derelict garage and switched off the engine. A rime of slushy ice clung like dirty scum to the edge of the salt marsh where I could just make out the humps of mallard curled into themselves for the night. Beyond lay the dark and unrevealing mud over which the sea was creeping. Jack leapt into my mind on a wave of fear that made me jump, so that John jumped too, pulling me back against the seat.

'Having second thoughts?' Cockburn didn't turn round, had picked up the sudden movement, read it right.

There had to be something I could say, the right words to stop this. 'Look,' I began, 'I don't know what you've got in mind, but is this necessary?' That wasn't right. Not for Cockburn. I had to find the code that could access not compassion nor morality, for he possessed neither, but his intellect; something that would amuse or challenge, flatter that gross ego.

I had run out of clever. All I could think of was Jack and my own fear of dying. The two were knotted together and I knew instinctively that if I tried using either of them to touch Cockburn what they'd access would be his sadism.

There was nobody else around: no bait-diggers returning from the open mud, no wind-surfers packing up their giant butterfly sails; nobody who might wonder what a car was doing parking this late in the day.

Cockburn was fiddling about with something on the seat beside him. 'Necessary – and interesting.' He swivelled round and leant comfortably on the deep upholstery. 'Life is a fantasy, Mig. Why should dying be any different? Hold her.'

John grabbed my good arm and clamped his fingers round my face. As Cockburn leant over the back of his seat I tried to get my feet up high enough to kick at him. There was a lot of struggling and hollering and heavy breathing before Cockburn emptied the contents of his trusty syringe into the soft skin between the middle fingers of my right hand. This time there wasn't any drenching smell, nor the sudden capitulation of consciousness. There was nothing.

'You needn't hold your breath,' said Cockburn, releasing his grip on my hand. 'It doesn't work that quickly.'

John relaxed his hold on my jaw but kept one leg across mine until Cockburn judged it dark enough for us to leave the car. Headlights from occasional traffic strafed the hedge of dead hogweed between the road and the footpath some 10ft below, and I made an attempt, just before the path branched off to the seawall, to break free, but it didn't work. Cockburn had rewound the scarf about my mouth and neck and was holding it like a leash. Any violent movement tightened it until I could hardly breathe. He waited until we were well on to the seawall before he gave me a bit of slack.

When we got level with the burnt-out hide I expected them to stop, for some reason, but we carried on past and as if reading my thoughts, Cockburn said 'Not here, Mig, it won't happen here.'

His voice sounded excessively loud in the silence.

As we neared the marsh John's breathing became the shunting of a steam engine beside my ear, and his fingers seemed to be sinking below the flesh on my arm as if he was being welded to me. If I struggled he would be fused into me for ever more. The idea was so awful that I shrank rigidly into myself to put some space between his flesh and mine, and the video tape's sharp corners reminded me it was still tucked into the sling.

We slithered down the seawall onto the river foot path which was still underwater from the previous tide. The nearer we got to the river the more the wind burnt into my skin, and into my brain, a scalding faucet of sound through which Cockburn's voice boomed and reverberated until I thought my ear drums would split. I peered at his face in the gloom. It was pink and beautiful, a plump cushion that I wanted to lay my face on. I leaned forward towards his lips, watching their supple movement as they shaped the deep oily sounds that slid like eels out of his mouth, each one fondled on its way by the glistening muscle of his tongue: 'Lysergicaciddiethylamide' sang his mouth. I didn't understand the meaning but they were wonderful words.

And then he was gone.

The List

I was on the edge of the river, looking down into the tide insisting its way upstream. Something was wrong. Afraid, I looked round for Cockburn whose absence I found far more ominous than his presence, and then back at the water. It was flowing in jerks, paroxysms of solid movement between the black lips of the river. Above it, on the opposite bank, the white tongue of beach lolled in the on-coming sea. Everything around me was swelling and dilating, the black banks of mud sucking me in like a greedy mouth. I started to run, wrenching my feet out of the gobbling ooze only to feel them clamped again. On my knees I looked up to get my bearings and the lights from the harbour hit me full in the face, their dazzling spears skimming across the bay in an endless fusillade of colour, pinning me to the mud like skewers in meat.

The lights radiated around me, then shot away until they appeared like train tracks across the sea, inviting me to follow. I tried to get up out of the glop but as soon as I got to my feet the treacherous lights dissolved, then amorphously flooded back around me, playing on my body. I left it to be consumed in the orange and gold striations, knowing that I'd gone mad and was totally isolated from the world; there was no world left; there was no me. Only this thing shrinking beneath the roof of a toothless chewing night, drowning me in its icy saliva.

These things I recall are sieved, moments that clung to my conscious mind like litter caught in a wire mesh fence. The rest slipped through and are gone.

The lights changed to faces, flying at me through the darkness, and on into my skull. They were warped and staring; thyroid eyes bolting at me with unimaginable speed; leprous, grinning, sneering faces soundlessly shooting into my closed eyes. Somebody said 'Draw them' and it sounded like my mother but it was also the artist Artemesia Gentileschi, although I didn't understand how. As each face zoomed into view I tried to slow it, to note its special features so that I could record them. They dissolved before they could get into my head and then they simply stopped coming. I pleaded with my mother to come back, but she couldn't. My cries became the sobbing of water around my body, and I hauled myself up. Birds flapped all around me, their wings hissing 'The list' before they wheeled away, so I followed them, looking for a place to lie down out of the on-coming tide, and in the squeaky sharp glasswort curled up foetus-like and began:

A for Garrett Anderson, B for Elizabeth Blackwell, C for Curie . . .

. . . the lights had sneaked across the bay and drawn in close behind me. I shrank, becoming smaller and smaller, knowing the lights were just waiting . . .

. . . Desdemona, Dworkin, Dulcie . . .

. . . my body was swelling and the lights were becoming tiny in comparison, although they almost pressed my skin they were so close. I curled in tighter, terrified at the distance between my head and the earth . . .

. . . E for Crystal Eastman, F for Friedan, G for . . .

174

. . . the lights ebbed and waned, sneaking up, retreating, as the list proceeded. Sometimes they brought faces with them but they disintegrated before I could see them properly.

And then everything became still, except me, chattering and shaking in the fleshy nest of purple marsh plant. And then even I became still.

If I stayed like that nothing would happen, nothing like when I moved because something was digging into my ribs, and then the purple plants became veins and arteries and the whole marsh was a wriggling, pumping bloody thing. I whispered the list endlessly into the wet placenta, each woman's name a votive to secure my tenure in the dark, freezing womb.

Billy Dawson's dog

Frederick Cockburn didn't fail. I have to make that clear because it is dangerous to underestimate men like him. They never found him, and John was missing for two years before his death from some wasting disease revealed his identity to the owners of the private nursing home where Cockburn had stashed him. That was a curious thing, somebody like Cockburn 'taking care' of John in that way: I wouldn't have been surprised if John's remains had been found on the dump near the reserve, or washed up by the sea. Maybe Cockburn felt for him like you do a stupid but loyal dog that's a danger to everybody else but loves you. I never heard Cockburn speak to him in the same tone that Catterell used. Money for John's upkeep apparently arrived regularly from various parts of Europe, always in British currency, but as soon as John died it stopped coming. The network was alive and well, despite the loss of Pope, two of his minions on the Force, a chemist, a solicitor and a town hall executive. Pope didn't get as long as I'd have liked, but long enough to see him into unhealthy old age.

I had thought Catterell was cunning, but he was just

following orders he hadn't been competent enough to carry out. Even had he not died I think Cockburn would have supervised what was meant to be my denouement, and it was not down to poor planning that I didn't bow out when he wanted me to. It was down to the extraordinary coincidences that weave like tangled telephone wires through our lives – that and Billy Dawson's dog.

Probably the same men who were horsing around in the Gun and Hunter when I last visited it were responsible for Billy's black labrador Flossie getting out of the back garden at closing time. Anyway, somebody let her out and Billy had her ideas who it was. 'Stupid sods,' she said. Flossie couldn't resist the attraction of the reserve at night with its promise of complacent rabbits and opportunist foxes going about their business unhindered by human intrusion. She'd bolted across the road and headed for the deeps, where she found me.

Later I realised I had been out there for about eight hours, even though then it seemed longer. Cockburn had rightly planned on me either drowning or dying of hypothermia, and if Flossie hadn't gone hunting, one of them would have been right. When she stuck her slimy nose in my face my shriek sent her slithering backwards through the water logged plants in shock. I'd risked opening my eyes for the first time in hours only to find death with long trails of saliva hanging from its jaws. Fortunately for me, curiosity got the better of her and she crept back, sniffing cautiously in case I turned out to be dangerous, and that was when I smelt her.

'Daisy!' Good old wet dog smell it was, and I tried to click my tongue in a mouth rigid with the cold.

She crept closer and I raised my hand. She sussed it out with her nose and then gave it a single lick. Her choke chain was dangling and I hooked a finger into it, and didn't let go. She didn't like it, but eventually she succumbed and stood beside me until somebody told her different.

By midnight Billy was worried enough to get her torch and come stomping through the reserve calling for Flossie, torch in one hand and her late husband's shotgun in the other. It was a pity Cockburn hadn't stayed around long enough to watch my antics because she might have used the shotgun on him, and that would have saved me from thinking about him as often as I do.

When Flossie heard her mistress calling she jumped up and would have run off but for my fingers in her chain. She howled her predicament across the echoing marsh, and the beam of the torch pierced the footpath from the seawall. There were more calls and canine responses, and then Billy Dawson was bending over me with a 'Christ Almighty!'

She dragged me as far as the seawall, grumbling to herself about her prolapse, and then looped the dog lead she'd brought round my wrist, hooked the other end into Flossie's collar and told her to stay. She kept telling both of us she'd be back and not to move, she'd be back and 'Bloody hell, what a life!'

She was back before the ambulance, with a blanket and a bottle of brandy which was as much for her as it was for me. She wrapped the blanket around me and hugged me to her, chanting a litany of comfort interjected with references to the lassitude of the modern police (of which her late husband had been the best member ever), the ambulance service, and punctuated with the glugging of the upturned bottle. I couldn't drink the stuff: it tasted like acid and for a dreadful moment I thought she was trying to poison me. Her hands and face were green and purple and the blanket felt like a straight-jacket. When I struggled to get free she let me go. 'Nothing to be afraid of,' she said, looking afraid herself. 'It's only Billy.'

I tried to tell her what had happened, but it came out as gibberish, about naked bodies and dead bodies, flying faces and women's names, and all the time she kept saying 'There, there, pet, you're safe now.'

'Nobody's safe,' I said finally, pushing away her hands.

She pulled her coat tighter around her middle and shivered. She must have forgotten to put on gloves; the nails of her manicured hands were the colour of stale blood in the lights from the torch that lay on her lap. 'I suppose you're right,' she said.

She insisted on going with me in the ambulance, regaining her self-possession when the police tried to dissuade her – 'What about your dog?' one of them asked.

'You take her back,' said Billy. 'Tell my daughter to give the lads a drink.'

The policeman and the ambulance driver exchanged a look that said 'Women!'

Billy winked at me as she plonked herself down on the opposite bed. 'Coppers! My old man was on the Force for 30 years and a fat lot of good it did him. My son's a bloody deputy Chief Constable and he'll probably die early like his dad.'

Everything was still a funny colour and I shut my eyes. The ambulance woman gave up trying to persuade me to lie down and started questioning Billy, dropping her voice so I wouldn't hear. Billy wasn't so discreet: 'Suicide, my arse! Somebody tried to kill her out there a while back.'

At the hospital I refused a wheelchair. Now I was on my feet I wanted to stay there. Billy accompanied me right up to the door of the examination room. 'If you need me, sing out. I'm not going until I know you're alright.'

I said it was okay, if she'd just ring Sue for me she could get off home. 'Have you got a video?' I added.

For the first time she looked at me as if I really might be mad, but when I dragged the tape out of the sling she took it.

'Is it important?'

'It's what it's all about,' I told her.

Selected Short Story collections

WATER WINGS
Caroline Natzler
Finely crafted modern British tales
ISBN 0–906500–38–9

MOSAIC OF AIR
Cherry Potts
Science fiction and new perspectives on ancient myths
ISBN 0–906500–38–9

A NOISE FROM THE WOODSHED
Mary Dorcey
Lyrical, sensuous and very witty fiction. Winner of the
Rooney Prize for Irish literature (1990)
ISBN 0–906500–30–3

SACCHARIN CYANIDE
Anna Livia
Satirical, literary and hilarious by turns from a best selling
author.
ISBN 0–906500–35–4

STRANGER THAN FISH
J. E. Hardy
Pessimism, realism and romance.
ISBN 0–906500–32–X

Selected Novels

TOUGH AT THE TOP
Nicky Edwards
Norfolk, where a clever, neolithic lesbian comments on
20th century troubles.
ISBN 0–906500–45–1

HATCHING STONES
Anna Wilson
Brilliant, tough dystopia about genetic engineering.
Ms Wilson's third novel
ISBN 0–906500–39–7

Selected Feminist Theory

FOR LESBIANS ONLY: A Separatist Anthology
ed. Sarah Hoagland & Julia Penelope
More than 70 contributors in a classic covering fifteen years of lesbian activism principally in North America. Never fails to initiate discussion.
ISBN 0–906500–28–1

Selected Poetry collections

NOTHING WILL BE AS SWEET AS THE TASTE
Elana Dykewomon
Ironic, intimate, politically savvy and sexy by turns.
ISBN 0–906500–57–5

LIGHTNING ON MY TONGUE
Tina Kendall
Black, British, Lesbian and always skillful.
ISBN 0–906500–50–8

SOFT ENGINEERING
Kate Foley
First collection from the winner of the 1993 Margot Jane Memorial Poetry prize.
ISBN 0–906500–51–6

PASSION IS EVERYWHERE APPROPRIATE
Caroline Griffin
Rife with the exhilaration to be found from a modern, British, Lesbian perspective.
ISBN 0–906500–34–6

Onlywomen Press, Radical Feminist Lesbian publishers (*since 1974*), produces fiction, poetry and feminist theory available from bookshops and libraries everywhere and also by mail-order.

This novel, *Burning Issues*, is the first in the new *OnlywomenCrime* list – we hope you enjoyed it. Please tell us what you think of our books – we'll give you a special mail-order discount if you reply before 1996.

✂ -

Crime Series Queries

How often do you read crime books?
Frequently ☐ occasionally ☐ rarely ☐

How did you discover Onlywomen Press books?
Friend's recommendation ☐ Seeing them on sale ☐
Reviews ☐

What kind of books do you think of first in association with Onlywomen Press? *[tick only one]*
Lesbian (anything) ☐ Feminist Theory ☐ Poetry ☐
Novels ☐ Short stories ☐ Science-Fiction/Fantasy ☐
Detective genre ☐

How much did you like this *OnlywomenCrime* title, *Burning Issues*?
Very much ☐ In parts ☐ Not at all ☐

Explain ....

....

Why did you buy (or borrow) it?
Friend's recommendation ☐ Intriguing cover design ☐
Interesting book review ☐

Please send me an Onlywomen mail-order catalogue.

I understand response to the Crime Series Queries entitles me to a 25% discount on an OWP title ordered from Onlywomen before 1996.

Name ....

Address..

....

....

Please post your replies to:
Onlywomen Press
40 St. Lawrence Terrace
London W10 5ST.